"A big story . . . a story of the West"
—*TRANSRADIO PRESS*

■ ■

HER NAME WAS VERA MAE

• • • and she had been around these dusty tank towns too long—working the two-bit rodeos and cozying up to suckers—like this fat tourist in the bar . . .

"Oh God," she thought, "I can con him and ditch him by nine-thirty, but what then? Sit in a hotel room. Get drunk and pass out. I'll be an old bag before I'm thirty . . ."

That was Vera Mae, fed-up, ripe for trouble when a lean ex-bronc rider named Lonnie drifted in from the desert . . .

"Prose that has the texture of a drawl . . . people warm and real . . . a corking climax."
—New York *HERALD TRIBUNE*

■■■■■■■■■■■ by RICHARD WORMSER

THE
LONESOME
QUARTER

BANTAM BOOKS

New York ■■■■■■■■■■■■■■■■■

THE LONESOME QUARTER

PART ONE

THE HOMESTEAD

OUT IN THE ARENA, they were calf-roping, and some of the boys were making good time. But Lon Verdoux had not come there to watch them calf-rope, though of all the rodeo events, it was about the only one that had anything to do with his present way of making a living. Until the bronc-riding started, he had no business there.

He stole a glance at the kids. He didn't want them to think he was spying on them, but he was their father, and he ought to see that they were doing all right. Well, they were. Mike was watching the calf-roping and trying to keep time with the three-buck watch Lon had given him on his birthday. June was kneeling backward on the seat, and he knew she'd lost interest in the rodeo and was looking over the ladies' clothes.

Just like Joan used to do.

It was a nice day. Over here on the coast side of the mountains, the sun was just warm enough. Some pretty good boys were singing "No Letter Today" over the loudspeaker system, and one of them had some new chords on the guitar that Lon had never heard before. On the track four quarter horses were lining up to run a heat, and the calf-roping was moving right along, not being bothered at all by the red-nosed roundup clown and his burro, who seemed to get in the way, but really didn't.

Lon was having a good time. He knew he shouldn't, but he was. It made him feel bad, but just being there with his kids, the sun on him, and the horses in the arena and on the track so pretty, well—it would take a smarter man than him to keep from feeling good.

1

Lon looked at the kids again, and just on the other side of June, a gal smiled at him. Lon caught himself smiling back, and then reached out and straightened the ribbon bow on one of June's braids, so the gal would know him for what he was, an attached man.

But she continued to grin at him. And then a fat man, on the other side of her, reached across and poked June in the ribs. Strangers were always fussing at June. You couldn't hardly blame them; there probably wasn't any prettier little girl any place. And the good little thing never minded; she was always polite. Lon sure hoped the fat man would leave Mike alone; you couldn't always count on his manners.

Fat Man said, "You gonna rope calves when you grow up, pahdneh?" He had on an embroidered shirt and frontier pants, with low shoes; his hat was brand-new. A rich dude. Maybe a banker or a lawyer, or anyway a big-business man. Lon hoped Mike would be wrapped up in one of his daydreams; the kid was still at an age when being strong and good-looking and all meant everything to him; he didn't understand how fat dudes were important people, and used to being treated accordingly.

June said, "Girls can't rope calves that way. They don't get strong enough to pick the calf up, even when they grow up."

The fat man thought this was very funny. He guffawed. He patted the gal with him on the leg so she wouldn't miss what June had said. It didn't sound as funny as all that to Lon, and maybe it didn't to the dude; Lon thought idly that he'd probably just picked the gal up, and any excuse to pat her just now was a good one. Rodeo gal.

The quarter horse racing went into its final, the last man roped his calf and made his time, and the clown brought out a little Arab stallion and made him do some tricks while they got the bucking stock ready. The quartet finished singing, and the announcer said somebody named

2

Red Martin was coming out on Steamboat in Chute One.

Whatever the kids were feeling, Lon's stomach felt cold and stiff as he watched Chute One. They were having trouble there. The rider was still up on the rails, and the horse was coming up to him, maybe six times a minute. Martin had better get into the saddle and start riding, or he'd have a dopey horse that left his fight in the chute. Maybe so it was safer that way, but there wasn't any money in it.

A hell of a way to make a living.

Now the chute opened, and Martin came out. There is always a Steamboat in every bucking string, and he is usually a roan, and this one was; a big hammerhead but even if he had had a smart head, a no-good horse, thick-legged and clumsy. There wasn't any spring in those legs ever, and now Steamboat was mad and stiff-legging it, and Martin was having himself a time. His hat flew off, showing red hair, and long before time was called Martin took a roll off the right side of Steamboat and kept on rolling.

The roan was hurt enough by the roweling he'd gotten and by the bucking strap not to come after him. The pickup men hazed him toward the exit chute, and they started getting a horse ready in Chute Four, and Lon looked at the kids.

They were just watching, and Mike was playing with his shiny watch again. June was more interested in this than she'd been in the calf-roping, but not too much. They weren't pale and they weren't sick, and it was going to be all right.

Lon wanted to tell somebody all that, but nobody here knew him, which was why he'd driven this long ride—and one spark plug not too good—because it would not look right, him going to a rodeo just now . . .

Fat Man poked June again. He sure liked poking girls, any age; he'd rested his right hand on that gal's frontier pants now. Lon was beginning to dislike the fellow. Fat

3

Man said, "That the way they ride broncs on yore range, buckaroo?" speaking like a comedian on the radio making fun of Western programs.

June never got a chance to answer. Mike put his watch away, and let his breath out, just as Lon had heard himself do a lot of times when there was something mean to be done. Mike said, "Of course not, Mister. We ride horses to gentle 'em, not to amuse fat dudes. An' quit pokin' my sister."

Lon said, "Mike, you watch those manners," as sharp as he could, because he wanted to laugh. Fat Man got red and then he got white again, and he looked at Lon and maybe he decided Lon'd make something of it if he talked back to Mike. But Lon wouldn't have; ten-year-old boys shouldn't get fresh to grownups, no matter what.

Then Lon saw that the girl was having a hard time of it. She looked like she was going to bust pretty soon.

A black-haired Indian-looking turtle was coming out of Chute Four on a gray they called Dynamite—there was always a Dynamite, too,—and June had lost all interest in the bucking again, and was wriggling around, restlessly.

Mike said, "Look, Pop, that rider's hooked his spurs," and he was right, the fellow riding had given up and was hanging on with his hooks in a cinch. The pickup men were closing in.

Lon could go home now. Or, at least, to the hotel room he'd rented. It wasn't good for kids to do too much in a day, and they'd driven since six that morning to get to this roundup. He—

Something would have to be done about June's wriggling. He swallowed, and said, "Honey—"

The gal on the other side of June stood up. "How's about you and me powdering our noses, sister?"

It was sure nice of her. Lon guessed she hadn't had to be a mind reader to know what June needed, or what a fix it always put him in. Fat Man, on the gal's other side,

4

looked kind of sore about it, but that was the gal's own problem. She looked able to handle it.

June stood up as good as she always was and took the gal's hand. Lon said, "You mind the lady, now," but that was to encourage the gal; June didn't need it. They went by Mike and then Lon, and the gal's tight saddle pants brushed his knee . . .

Manners insisted that he talk to Fat Man while the dude's gal was taking care of June. He said: "Anything you want to know about the rodeo, Mister, just ask. I used to work rodeo myself, before I settled down."

Fat Man was trying to be agreeable, too. "Local boy?"

"No," Lon said. "East sider—from back on the edge of the desert." He laughed. "Land in here costs just about as much an acre as my whole ranch is worth."

Fat Man offered cigarettes. Lon took one, and struck a match on his thumbnail for the two of them. "Nice of the lady to help out with my little girl."

The dude said, "Sure," uncertainly. Then he added quickly. "Hold my seat for me, will you, buckaroo? I'm going to get a beer."

It was some trouble to let the fat body out, but they managed it. When he was gone, Mike said reflectively, "When you were travelin' around, Pop, what'd you used to enter in?"

Lon said, "Depends. When a rider brought home money, he'd just go in for one, two things the next day. Maybe calf-roping and bronc-riding. After a dry spell, you'd put your name down for everything you could afford. One time I borrowed on my saddle from the fella that was promotin' the show, and ran my name right down the list—includin' the wild horse race and the cow-milking, bull-riding and—if I remember right—I tried to ride the clown's trick mule for five dollars, too."

Mike said, "Should think you'da been sore."

His father told him, "I don't remember. Don't remember the last half of the day at all. Woke up in a stall on some hay, with sixty dollars in prize money, over what I'd borrowed. But only way I know how I got there is hearsay."

Mike laughed. There was no danger of him ever doing any damn-fool thing like that. He was all rancher. All the time climbing up the canyons, looking for springs, trying to figure out some way to irrigate the ranch. He was the solemnest ten-year-old that Lon had ever known, which was funny, because it didn't seem to come from either side of the family.

Mike said, "Here comes June and that lady. Pop—"

Lon said, "Yeah?" with some caution. He was shy of questions; they made him wish he'd gone to school more.

"Pop, I don't like that fat man."

Lon sighed. This was easy. "You don't have to, Mike. Maybe so, though, he'd be all right if you saw him in what Tommy calls his natural habitat."

"Well, I'm glad I don't have to like him," Mike said. "The lady's pretty, though. His wife."

Lon swallowed. An honest father would probably explain that the lady wasn't Fat Man's wife. And if it was done right, it might not start a lot of other questions that Lon wouldn't be able to answer. But June was wriggling back in, followed by the gal, and there wasn't any use saving the speech till later; just let it die.

June was bubbling, her eyes bright and her cheeks pink. They had had bottles of pop, and they had weighed themselves, and the lady's name was Vera Mae and—smell, Pop —Vera Mae had put perfume behind June's ears—

Lon smiled and laughed. He said to the gal, "You combed her hair, too. I thank you."

"Kindly," Vera Mae added. "June has lovely hair. Where did my ch—friend go?"

"Get himself a beer," Lon said.

Vera Mae said, "Move over, Mike," and sat down between the kids.

Mike said, "June told you my name."

"Right the first time." She nodded toward the arena.

6

"Bull-riding just start?" Out there a gray-haired cowboy had himself straddled on a yellow Brahma. He gave it a pretty good ride, and jumped clear without the pickup men. "Duke Holloway," the girl said. "About as good a rider as follows the rodeos."

"I'll bet he's not as good as Pop was when he traveled around," June said.

"I'll bet he is," Lon said. Something in the way he said it made the girl laugh. He asked her, "You ride?"

"Not buckers," she said. "I'm a roper. When they have mixed-team roping, Duke and I work together. And I do some trick riding."

"You must be pretty good."

"I'd never get first money at Pendleton," Vera Mae said. "Or any kind of money at Madison Square. But I can catch a head about four out of five and a heel, one out of three."

"That's not bad," Lon said. "You got no call to run yourself down."

"I wasn't," she said. "Hello, big boy."

Fat Man didn't look pleased about finding her sitting between Mike and June. He stood there a second, having trouble balancing in the squeezed space, and then Vera Mae switched, fast, and ended up on the other side of June. Fat Man sat down again, holding his beer, and put his hand back on her knee. This put him in a good humor, and he asked Mike, "Them the kind of cows you-uns run?"

Mike looked at the Brahma bulls out in the arena. A fellow was riding a gray one, and the three already ridden were still larruping around the field, refusing to use the runout gate. "Naw," Mike said.

"But you've got a ranch," Vera Mae said. "June told me. Over by the desert."

"Just a quarter-section," Lon said.

Fat Boy perked up. "Hundred and sixty acres," he said. "That could be worth a lot of money. Land, in this state, is going for forty dollars an acre, and up."

7

Lon laughed. "Up where I live it ain't. Ten bucks an acre'd be a big price. Country runs about one cow to thirty acres. But I got a Forest Service right to run sixteen head, and with luck, I make out."

The dude was really interested now. It was like Lon must remember to tell the kids; just because a man was fat and had bad manners, you oughtn't to throw off on him. Fat Man probably made as much in a month as Lon made all year, working hard, and it was probable, if you could get him to put his mind to it, he could tell a brush-whicker like Lon how to do better with what he had.

"My name's Dutcher," the Fat Man said. "I'm in the hardware business." Out in the arena, steer-stopping was going on, and nobody was much interested. Some fellows were trying to line up some hot-bloods with flat saddles on the track, but they were having trouble. "I sell logging equipment," Dutcher said, "and so on. What's this about the Forest Service?"

"The national forest around my place is all logged over and thinned out," Lon told him. "But there's pretty good grazing. So they give me an allotment. I can run sixteen head on the forest and my land throwed together. And—"

The gal was stirring. "There's nothing more on the program I want to see, big boy," she said. "Let's go have a drink."

Mr. Dutcher's eyes got kind of glassy. He squeezed the leg he had been resting his hand on, and said, "Good idea. Maybe we'll see you, cowboy." He looked at the kids, and his voice got on that silly radio kind of manner again. "Don't go ridin' no outlaws, now, young-uns."

When they were gone, June stared at nothing for a long time. Then she made a pronouncement. "I like Vera Mae," she said.

Lon laughed. What she meant was just the same as Mike when he said he didn't like Mr. Dutcher. "You kids had enough rodeo?" he said.

8

They thought. "I want to go back to the hotel and take a bath," June said.

Mike promptly agreed. Lon said, "Well, all right. Two baths in a day never hurt. If you're good you can have another one tomorrow morning."

Behind the stands they ran ahead of him, looking for the car, discussing what they were going to do in the tub. Mike was going to put a matchstick on a cake of soap and sail it for a boat, and June was going to put her head under water and blow bubbles.

Lon felt like singing. It had come off all right. He had found out what he wanted to know; they weren't afraid of horses, buckers meant no more to them now than—before. He could stay on the homestead, and stick to what he knew best. And besides—nobody from home had seen him at the rodeo; he'd gotten away with it. Everything was just fine, for the first time in a long time.

CHAPTER II

IT WAS a good bar for dudes, Vera Mae thought. Copper-metal walls made everybody look healthy and sunburned. They made old Duke down the bar look dark as a saddle, and what they did to Turk, leaning next to Duke, was almost to make him disappear in the gloom, just a hat and a shirt with no face in between.

She told the mark, "You see that fellow down there with the white hat on? We call him Turk. Want to know why?"

For all the fat crowding his eyes half-shut, his lips were thin and cruel. He said, "Shoot, pahdneh. Want another dose of this snake-pizen?"

She nodded. She no longer wanted to tell him about Turk. But she had to go on talking. He hadn't bought her dinner yet. He hadn't been steered past the store where there was the silver bracelet that could be taken back for half-price tomorrow. He hadn't— "He's an Indian," she said. "Osage, I think. Anyways, he's from Oklahoma. And one time, in Santa Fe, they didn't want to serve him a drink."

The bartender put another old-fashioned in front of her, and the lop-ear said, " 'Cause he was drunk?"

"No. It's against the law to sell drinks to Indians."

"Sure," the thin lips said helpfully, "it makes 'em go crazy. Firewater."

Oh God. And it wasn't six-thirty yet. Vera Mae figured, I can con him and ditch him by nine-thirty—well, ten—but then how about the rest of the evening? Sit in a hotel room. Get drunk and pass out. I gotta cut down on drinking, I'll be an old bag before I'm thirty— "So the bartender says, 'Pardon me, but are you an Indian?' and Turk—his real name's Dick Lacekin—says, 'No, I'm a Turk. I got my union card in the cigarette blender's union right here some place.' And with that the bartender—he was almost a blond —rears back and starts spouting something that musta been Turkish."

Under the bar a fat hand had come to rest on her saddle pants, halfway up from the knee. She dropped her own hand over it, to keep him interested and restrained both, and felt the coolness and size of the diamond in his ring. A fat mark. "So Turk just looks at him, while the rest of us get ready for fireworks, and Turk says, 'I can tell from your accent you're from North Turkey. Well, damn you, suh, when you speak to a South Turk, call him cunnel,' and he walks out."

The lop-ear thought this over. "So he didn't get his drink."

"That's right, Daddy," Vera Mae said. "I gotta go to the john." Behind her, Fat Eyes was chuckling. That was the way to handle him, maybe. Just use a half-dirty word now and then, so he'd know she was his kind. Well, better luck tomorrow. They were working their way up north, she and Duke and a dozen of the other boys and gals. She stopped by Duke. "Hey, if you're going to the committee office, put me down for steer-stopping, will you?"

Duke said, "The prize ain't worth gettin' dusty for."

"That's why there won't be many out. That's why I'm liable to get some money."

Turk said, "It's a long an' weary world, friends."

"G'wan, Indian, you're drunk."

Coming out of the ladies' room she was facing the lobby of the hotel instead of the bar. She had to stop and think, and then she remembered you turned right for the bar; the rest rooms did double duty, you could get to them from bar or lobby either, only from the bar—

She was feeling her drinks more than she'd thought, and she crossed the lobby to the coffee shop, and drank a cup black and hot enough to scorch the roof of her mouth. She'd better hurry, the mark would be getting impatient, but why hurry; what else was there for him to do in this jerkwater town? The local gals, in their white blouses and dark blue slacks or black skirts, would not care to be seen with him, and they wouldn't know what to do with him if they got him.

But she knew.

Sorry for yourself, Vera Mae? 'Cause you got no call to. You bought just what you've got, and you like it. Got a horse, standing pretty out at the fairgrounds eating and his feed bill paid. Got a saddle and a rope, a real linen rope, good boots, clothes—and you've got some of the swellest friends anybody ever had. Duke, Turk—all cowboys.

She couldn't remember the time when that wasn't what she wanted. The other girls had thought she was crazy because she'd always swap a Greta Garbo or a Ginger Rogers picture for a Gene Autry or a Bill Boyd, and she'd gone around talking with a German accent for weeks after seeing Marlene Dietrich in "Destry Rides Again."

First, she'd hung around the riding academies on the

11

edge of Griffith Park, and sometimes if you kidded them, the men'd let you ride free on weekdays, when there weren't many customers and the plugs—only she thought they were wonderful, real cow ponies—were in danger of going Monday-morning lame. From there it had been just a step to being taken to the Rancho or the Palace Barn for dancing, and it was after one of those dances that one of the fellows had taken her back to the barn, and a bale of hay. From then on, she could ride all she wanted to. Good horses, too, out in the Valley, in Reseda and Northridge, where they'd have parties in the tackrooms, and hardly anybody ever went into the house at all unless it was to powder her nose.

Swell people, guys and gals who rode double for Republic and Universal and Tim McCoy or just rode, as henchies and posses in pictures, or maybe were wranglers or took care of the stock for the actors. She was only sixteen, but they took her right into the gang, and she almost got a Guild card herself, only her folks found out how little she'd been to school, and raised hell . . .

She came out of the coffee shop, and moved slowly toward the bar. She looked down. Her boots needed a shine; there was a stand over in the corner by the barbershop. Only, how long would a mark wait, nursing a drink at a bar?

She'd gone back to school, then, and only seen her friends on Friday and Saturday nights, and daytimes Saturday and Sunday, and it was one Saturday night when they'd all gone down to Pico to hear a fellow that used to be at the Rancho play the guitar that she met Kenny and they went down to Tijuana the next day and got married.

Vera Mae, snap out of it, people will stare at you, standing in the middle of a lobby this way, not knowing which way to turn. Get back in the bar, and go to work.

Then she saw the rancher she'd been talking to out in the grandstand come out of the restaurant. He was carry-

12

ing a tray, his run-over boots wobbling some on the carpeted floor. Taking dinner up to his kids . . .

Lonnie Verdoux.

She walked over and punched the elevator button for him, and all at once she knew that Fat Stuff was going to have a long, lonely wait in the bar.

CHAPTER III

THE TRAY was too heavy, and the plates were too hot. The gray-haired lady in the hotel restaurant had been real pleased to be fixing a supper for two little children to eat in their hotel room. She'd put a plate of pickles and celery and olives on from the regular dinner, saying the hotel could spare them, and she'd put all the hot food in fancy plates that had boiling water under them, and the result was, Lon didn't know could he make it to the elevator and press the button and get in and close the door and—

A voice said, "Let me help you, cowboy," and there was the gal called Vera Mae, punching the button for him and steadying his elbow all at one time.

"Thanks," he said. "I didn't think I was going to make it."

"It takes practice walking on carpets in high heels." Vera Mae pulled the elevator door shut, and when he told her "four" pressed the button. "I'll go along as a sort of a convoy."

"You're a nice girl," he said. He heard himself adding, "Pretty, too."

She didn't answer him. Or his big mouth. Man with two kids and no clear way of making any money ought to learn he wasn't no big catch of a beau.

The elevator stopped, and he got out. "Sure," Vera Mae said. "And your wife doesn't understand you."

He stopped, the metal tray burning his hand from the boiling water. He swung around to face her. A bottle of milk nearly went over, and Vera Mae caught it with her hand, straightened it.

"My wife's dead," he said. "And I wasn't trying to get fresh." Then he grinned. "It just comes natural, I guess. I don't have to try."

"I'm sorry," she said. "And you weren't fresh. But these back-country hotshots—take the kid to the rodeo, and leave the old lady home to feed the chickens."

Lon said, "We don't keep chickens," and then at the look on her face, burst into laughter. She had to hold one edge of the tray for him, or he would have spilled the whole thing; they stood in the hotel corridor, holding the tray between them, laughing like fools. Then she said, "Ouch," as the hot water reached her, and he had the whole tray again.

"Lady downstairs broke her neck trying to make the supper nice," he said. He started toward the room, walking careful. But Vera Mae trailed along.

"Young lady?" she asked. She twisted the knob of the door he nodded at.

"Well, not so young," he said. "Said she had a boy about my age, about forty, and me, I'm only thirty-one. Those kids are going to wash clear away."

There was no sign of the children in the bedroom, but the splashing noises from the closed bathroom door were a pretty good sign that neither of them had drowned. Lonnie set the tray down on the bench, and kind of braced himself to go in there and lay down the law, but Vera Mae was still watching him.

She grinned and put a finger to her lips. She looked about Mike's age herself as she snatched up the two glasses of ice water from the tray and tiptoed to the bathroom door, holding her lips together real straight so as not to

14

make any noise. But she didn't need to worry; Mike and June wouldn't have heard a powder blast.

She whipped the door open, and threw the water out of the glass in two expert shots. The kids sounded like they'd been bird-shot. Then June shrieked, "Vera Mae!" and Mike's voice, a little deeper, followed after a second.

"You two come out," Vera Mae said. "And I mean dry. Your dad's worn out from lugging a ton of food up to you." She shut the bathroom door and winked at Lon; then she went over to the tray and raised the shiny metal covers.

"It's what they asked for," Lon said defensively. "Club sandwiches and milk and French pastry. God knows where they heard of 'em."

"Sounds all right to me," Vera Mae said. "Bread and meat and raw vegetables. Isn't that what they're supposed to eat?"

"I guess so," Lon said. He tried to keep his voice from sounding so gloomy. "But the PTA ladies came up one time and raised hell with me. I dunno. I'd gone to a lot of trouble to get tomatoes, too."

The kids burst out of the bathroom like a bull out of a chute. They looked pretty good, except their hair was still wet. Vera Mae went and got two towels; she threw one to Lon, and grabbed June herself. He started rubbing Mike's head; he felt a little like he'd been kicked in the stomach.

She looked up, once, and said, "I'm not being bossy, am I?"

He said, "Naw, but the gent you were with—"

She stared at him across June's head, across Mike's held down in his lap. "Yeah, Lon?" He didn't even know she knew his name; June must have told her.

"Nothing," he said. He moved his lips very deliberately; he wasn't going to mumble. "I just thought he might be waiting some place."

"Let him wait," she said. Because her voice wasn't pretty

now, it was the first time he noticed how nice it had been before. Then the bells came back into it. "No," she said. "Duke's downstairs—you know, I pointed him out to you; he's with an Indian rider, an Okie we call Turk, he's got a white hat on." She let go of June, gave the little girl a pat on the backside and sent her toward the bed. Then she went over to the flimsy little table where the kids had been drawing houses, and took the hotel pen and a sheet of paper. She wrote something and put it in an envelope.

"G'wan down to the bar," she said, "and give this to Duke. And have yourself a drink. But just one."

"I gotta get the kids—"

"Woman's work," she said. "If you don't trust me, send the chambermaid in."

"The chambermaid?" he asked. Then he took a breath. "Listen, don't be snippy. I trust you okay, it's just—well—seems to me it's my job to get the kids bedded down."

"Pardon me for intruding."

He heard himself shouting. His face, he knew, was getting red, the way it used to. "I told you not to be so snippy. I'd like to have a drink! I'm going!"

Then she was laughing at him, and he was aware of four huge eyes staring at him from the pillow. "Loud, ain't he?" Vera Mae said, and the four eyes got normal size again. "Send the chambermaid in anyway. I want her to do something for me. That's the lady who makes the beds, country boy."

"I know what a chambermaid is," Lon said, he hoped without yelling. This was the most irritating female he'd seen in a long time. He sure liked her.

And so did the kids, from the way they were grinning as she advanced on 'em in the bed, a sandwich plate in one hand, and a bottle of milk in the other . . .

It was funny, walking into a bar that way, not a care in the world. The riders she called Duke and Turk were there all right; he pushed up next to them and told the bar-

16

tender, "Whatever these gents are having, and an old-fashioned for me." He laid a five spot on the bar, and it was a long time since he'd done that. But there comes a time when a fellow can't be a piker much longer. He'd been watching pennies an awful long time.

The rodeo riders were looking at him. Seeing he didn't want a fight, the gray-haired one, Duke, said, "Well, thanks, Mister."

"Gotta note for you," Lon said. He handed it over. "From Vera Mae."

Duke took the hotel envelope. "In the movies, a fella always says excuse me before he reads a letter. It never made any sense to me."

Turk said, "Be a funny kind of guy that'd not read a letter. What would people send him one for, if they didn't want him to read it?"

The bartender brought three drinks and set them down. "Thanks, Mister," Turk said. Duke was reading the letter. Turk held Lon's eyes, and raised his drink.

Still puzzling over the note, Duke raised his glass without looking up.

"Here's to you, and thanks." He drank his drink in one gulp, and said to Turk. "This here's Lon Verdoux. Turk Lacekin. Me, I'm Duke Holloway. Vera Mae says we're to look him over."

"That Vera Mae," Turk said. He took the note from Duke, said, "Excuse me, gentlemen," and read it. He read a good deal faster than his older friend. "Yep, that's what she says. Lon, consider yourself looked over." He laid some money on the bar and said, "This one's on me."

"The hell it is," Duke said.

"You had the one last week," Turk said. Apparently they weren't arguing over buying the drink. Turk shoved back from the bar, and walked toward the front of the copper-colored place.

In the back, four guys, pale but in rodeo clothes, came out through a curtain and sat down on a little platform, two of them carrying guitars and the third one a squeeze-box. They were the same ones Lon had liked out at the fairgrounds. They began to sing "Red River Valley," and Duke bought three drinks out of Turk's money. "You ride any?" he asked Lon.

"Not in the last ten years," Lon said. "Me and a boy named Johnny Wheelwright traveled around some then. Southern California, Arizona, up into Colorado, and back here. I heard Johnny was still at it."

"Seems to me I heard the name," Duke said. "I couldn't be sure . . . It's a sucker kind of life. I'd like to drop a rope over my own cow sometime."

"Don't get me wrong," Lon said. "I ain't no cattle baron."

Duke laughed. "Don't get me wrong. I never took first money at Madison Square."

They both laughed. Lon said, "I got sixteen head, all told. Three horses to chase 'em on. Only way I make out is working for the government, summers."

"Forest Service?" Duke asked.

Lon nodded. "If I could turn over into about ten mares, I could make money."

Duke took a long swallow of his highball. "Never heard of anybody making money raisin' horses."

Lon said, "Well, I don't like to brag unless I have to, but I'd like to give her a try."

Turk came back and took up his waiting drink. "No trouble at all."

Duke asked, "You her husband?"

"No," Turk said. "Rodeo police. Told him he'd been seen with a suspect."

"That works real good," Duke said. "My turn to buy."

"I thank you," Lon said, "but I got to be upstairs. Got a couple of kids need me."

Duke laughed. "You'll have to fight us to get out of here. And me, I'm kind of stove-up, but Turk's a bad man to tangle with."

18

Turk shook his white hat. "Wouldn't say that." He thought a minute. "But Duke's right ingenious with himself, come a tussle. Remember once, in Redding, California, how—"

"What is this, anyway?" Lon asked. "You guys drunk, or just horsing around?"

"Show him the letter," Turk said. "Y'know, I got so much Turkish blood in me, I can't blush. So it does me real good to see somebody else get red in the face."

Duke thought a minute. "All right," he said. "Of course, Vera Mae'll lynch us."

He handed the sheet of hotel paper over, and Lon, still looking from one to the other of them, not sure this wasn't some sort of joke they played on country boys, took it. The bartender brought three more drinks, and took Duke's money.

Dear Duke:—

This'll be brought you by a guy named Lonnie Verdoux, who'll buy you a drink. Buy him one back, but don't get him drunk, cause I'm taking him out to supper. He is a nice guy with two kids and his wife is dead, and I don't think he's had much fun lately. Maybe if I do something for somebody else once in awhile, it'll change my luck, which sure needs it.

There's a fat faced jerk named Dutcher waiting for me in the bar. You or Turk throw him out. I'll see you.

V.

Lon grabbed for his drink, and never felt it go down his throat.

"Boy," Turk said. "Is he doing a good job of blushing!"

L ON FINISHED the last of his fried shrimp and pushed back from the table. "It runs good," he said earnestly. "Even in the end of September, when the wind's from the desert, she's never gone dry. Mike's after me to maybe put a dam on her, and run two, three feeder lines from other springs in, and irrigate maybe an acre of natural pasture. The SCS man told him that'd feed five, six cows, or two, three horses, but Tommy—he's the District Ranger up there—says it won't, that it'd take care of half that many. I dunno—" He broke off. Vera Mae was grinning at him.

He said, "I guess this is kinda dull. I'm sort of out of practice, taking a girl to dinner."

"I'm taking you out, but we'll argue that later. You used to be a ladies' man?"

Lon felt himself grinning foolishly. But he recovered. "I wouldn't say that. But when I was traveling around, I was more used to gals. Lord! I reckon those rodeo ladies have all settled down and are making homes now! That was ten years ago . . . It's why I'm so careful to try and do what Mike wants, if I can barely scrape up the money. I wouldn'ta left the homestead if my father hadn't been so set in his ways . . . He ran just about enough beef to feed us, and made his money cuttin' off the timber . . . Now it's all gone, and it's taken a hell of a lot of water and topsoil with it."

"So you're giving Mike a voice in how you run the ranch, even if he's only ten."

He nodded. The waitress came and took away their plates, and they ordered coffee. Vera Mae looked at him over the rim of her cup. "You're a good father."

"Well, they're good kids . . . I guess you're kind of curious about what kind of a man it is that'll go to a rodeo, and his wife only buried two months."

She looked down at her plate. Her hair was beautifully brushed, and the part went right down the middle, straight as if it had been drawn with a ruler. Doing up June's hair every morning had been an awful chore at first, and he'd been half-scared to send her to school when Easter vacation ended. Hadn't sent her, in fact, but the teacher thought that was on account of her mother. But finally he had decided he was being silly, and when she came home that night, she hadn't mentioned it, so the teacher or the other kids hadn't said anything.

He'd like to tell Vera Mae about it. She wouldn't either laugh or get all wet up around the eyes, like almost any other woman he'd ever known. And she'd understand how he couldn't even let Dot, down at the ranger station, know about his trouble over a little thing like hair.

She said, "Penny."

"I was thinking I like the way you do your hair."

"Why, cowboy!"

When he looked up, she was as red in the face as he'd gotten when Duke gave him the note. It gave him kind of a good feeling to be able to do that to her, but it was cruel to keep it up. He said, "You and Duke and Turk pretty close?"

She said, "Thanks . . . Well, Duke and me. Turk's a nice fellow to talk to, but all of a sudden he goes off and you don't see him for a year. Yes, last winter, I stayed in with Duke and his wife. They have a place in the San Fernando."

He said, "Oh," very carefully, because she was kind of uncomfortable, the way she could read what he was thinking.

Even so she read him this time. "No," she said. "I'm divorced . . . I'll tell you about it sometime—and—and unspoke for."

21

The waitress was coming over with the check. He said, "All right."

All in a rush the rest of it came out. "And I don't pick up suckers like that fat Dutcher unless things are awful rough."

The waitress gave him the check, but Vera Mae got it faster than anything he'd ever seen. "I asked you to dinner. And I meant it."

He shrugged. God knows, if he knew anything, Lonnie was a boy knew when not to argue with women. "It's better than borrowing from your friends. Duke or Turk."

Her eyes came clear open. "You see that?" she said. He had to bend forward to hear her. "Well—if you see that—I can tell you the rest. Kenny—my husband—went to prison. He cut a man."

"You got no call to be telling all this."

"I know that . . . I was going to divorce him anyway. So I went ahead with it. He was no good, Lon. And they caught him at it, he got two to ten years for mayhem. I heard he's in Arabia now, skinning cat . . . And I'll tell you the rest. I married him because he was the best bronc rider I'd ever seen."

"I couldn't stay on a rodeo bucker ten seconds," Lon said bravely, and got his reward; she started laughing again. She said, "Thanks, sister," to the waitress for the change, and left a tip and stood up. "Walk me out to the fairgrounds to look at my horse."

But outside he hesitated, and she said, "I told the chambermaid we wouldn't be back till about eleven; to sit with the kids till then. Let's walk, it isn't far out to the fairgrounds."

"My pickup is at the hotel."

"No, let's walk." She took his arm, and they turned right. The street was crowded, with the usual rodeo night crowd of any Western town; the shopkeepers and the clerks in the department stores and banks and utility companies, the foremen in the millwork plant had all put on

22

plaid shirts and saddle pants or levis; some of the men and women wore high-heeled boots, but most of the tight breeches ended disappointingly in low heels and laces.

Mixed up with the crowd were millworkers in their Sunday best and others in overalls and denim jackets, going up for the night shift. There were farmers and ranchers from around the countryside, there were a couple of dozen professional rodeo riders following the circuit, and there were some pickpockets and short-con workers—who also followed the circuit.

There was a merry-go-round set up at a wide corner, and kids whooped and yelled and dodged around underfoot, their faces smeared with chili and hot-dog mustard.

Lonnie nodded at one brat who had nearly collided with the solid rear end of a state policeman. "That kid's only about seven. Ought to be in bed."

Vera Mae laughed. "Stop being a professional father. You're a young man out with a girl."

"Well—" They had passed the lighted streets, were in the dark belt between town and the fairgrounds. The sidewalks ended, and he had to feel for the paving rather than watch it. He put his arm around Vera Mae's shoulders.

"That's better," she said. "I'd think I was losing my grip if you didn't try and cop a feel now and then."

"Don't talk so rough," Lonnie said. "You can't scare me. I heard all the words once, even if I don't know what they mean."

There was a light in each of the barns at the fairground, and a couple of patient watchmen walking the rounds, sniffing for fire. The smell of cows and horses came out of the first buildings they passed, and also a small whiff of pig. "Whoosh," Vera Mae said. "Why do pigs smell so much like pigs? You seen the twin palominos?"

"June went right to them," Lonnie said. "Just like Mike found the soil conservation exhibit." But they turned in at the fairground building anyway.

In a front stall a cream-colored mare stood drowsing,

but she shook off her tiredness when she saw she had visitors, and threw her head back proudly, her silver mane rippling. And she had something to be proud of: twin colts, as rare as human twins, and both of them a paler gold than hers, but with a dark skin promising they'd be the true palomino when they grew older, a color by definition the "shade of a newly minted gold piece."

A blue ribbon fastened to the front of the stall said, "Special Award, Palomino Mare with Twin Colts," but neither of them laughed at her as the two youngsters waded through the deep straw and began to nurse, pushing each other back and forth until each got a nipple.

"Golly," Vera Mae said, "I love horses. Everything about them, the way they look and the way they eat, and the way they smell . . . I've sure been around them a lot, and I never get tired of them."

"Did I tell you," Lonnie asked, "that I started to turn the ranch over into a horse ranch? Everybody says there's no money in it, but I wanted to try anyway."

"What happened?" Vera Mae asked. She smiled at the mare, and took his arm and guided him out into the night. They started toward the dark grandstand and the rodeo stock barns behind it.

"My stallion got away," Lonnie said. "Old Mulemouth."

"Got away? What'd he do, cut himself up on barb wire?"

"No," Lonnie said. "He just got away. He's running loose on the desert." He could feel her staring at him, somehow, though it was too dark to see her expression. He guessed maybe he ought to explain. "He was wild," he said. "There's a lot of wild horses around our country. Mostly just little broomtails, but sometimes a good mare gets away and runs with them, sometimes some rich man comes up and starts raising horses and gets tired of it and moves away and—"

"I've never seen wild horses," she said. "I mean really

24

wild, not this rodeo stock, but wild and not belonging to anybody."

They were past the grandstand and skirting along the corrals that held the roping steers and calves, the Brahma bulls. Ahead stretched the long stable where the riding stock slept; then off in the night, dust still rose from a corral where the broncs were put up.

"They aren't worth rounding up," he said again. "When I was a kid, they used to have big drives, round 'em up, break the best of 'em, shoot the rest; the broomtails were taking the country over. Now it's not so bad, there aren't so many. But there was this one—"

He stopped, because she'd stopped walking and was leaning into a box stall. A head came out to greet her. She stroked the horse's nose, and said, "Go on."

"Well, we called him Mulemouth. And most of the boys around there said there wasn't any such a thing, and some said he'd been seen, but it was always by somebody you couldn't count on. So—" He stopped again. "This is all mixed up. What do ya call your horse?"

"Brownie," she said. "He's seal brown, six years old, fifteen-three. And I want you to look at his near front leg, but later. First tell me."

He said, "I want to. I just want to get it straight in my mind first . . . We had these two kids, Mike and June, and they were wonderful. I wanted another, and Joan was favorable . . . But it ain't much of a ranch. People hear you're a rancher, and they think you're rich, but it's the last homestead anybody's hung on to, up there . . . Some of 'em went back to the government, and some big companies have bought up, for land and cattle or timber . .,. You can't hardly make out on a sagebrush quarter."

"It sure is mixed up, Lonnie . . . Take your time."

His hand ran down the horse's nose, and found her fingers. She hung on tight, and that made it easier, the pressure on his fingers like the kids', only different.

"So I took off, we have three horses, and I packed one

25

and rode one and left Joan the other to work the ranch. I was gone three weeks. Couldn't get nobody to help me, nobody believed, you see and— Anyway, I built a brush fence across a box canyon. Staked my mare in there, and rode out on the gelding, we call him Bob . . . Tracked him and tracked him—"

"This is in the desert?"

He said, "Yeah. There are high buttes there. The stallions get on 'em, and look out. I run off two studs, and they wasn't him. I rode two pairs of shoes right off Bob, and I tacked the third one on, and told myself when they were gone, I'd have to quit."

"How about food?" she asked.

"Joan and me jerked some beef. I still had some left. And Bob and me, we were both raised in that country, we can stand an awful lot of alkali . . . Lots of that water on the desert won't kill you, it just tastes bad . . . I picked up the track of this herd, and damn, the stud had big feet, and deep prints, like he was heavy . . . Coulda been some old truck horse somebody turned out, but I didn't think so . . . I stayed behind him drifting. By that time, I reckon I'd been on Bob so long, if they had smelled me, they'da thought I was a horse. But I'd shoot off a gun once in a while, to keep them moving. A fella told me once, if you keep them moving, they'll head for the rim of the desert, where a moving horse can eat and walk. You see, he had a bunch of mares about due to drop their colts, and that held him down. Even so, sometimes old mares'd drop out past me, they couldn't keep up. None of 'em was worth nothing, just broomtails. I wanted to see a colt, see if it was any better than its mama."

"You never got to see Mulemouth, then?" Still holding his hand, she ducked under Brownie's head, and came up facing him, close. Natural as if they'd practiced for a springtime, she relaxed against his shoulder, most of her weight on the stall door.

"Bob and me kept them moving so that Mulemouth

would have to stay in front, picking the way, finding feed and water. There was pretty good graze back where I'd left my mare, and anyway, a wild stud'll almost always stop and try and add a good mare . . . All of a sudden, he heard her whinnying, and the last six miles it was me and Bob right after him, and the mares scattering to hell and gone. When I pulled my trap, they all come up against it from outside, whinnying to papa. But he was in there with our Betsy, seventeen hands tall and prettiest horse I ever did see, golden buck with black mane and tail and four black legs. And in good shape, even then. A horse that could stand all that and still look good—"

"Money couldn't buy him," Vera Mae said.

"Naw. And you could always sell his colts. He was plenty mad, but not bronco-mad, not mad enough to kill himself, like some little ole wild studs've done . . . I went and got everybody I knew, and we got enough ropes on him to make him say uncle, and trucked him up the mountain and into a breaking corral I'd built, ten feet high and solid logs."

He stopped. Her cheek moved up against his for a second, and then away. She said, "I never heard anything like that. I never knew a cowboy didn't have something like that, a lost gold mine, or a wild horse that was really worth money, or a place in the desert where there is all the water you want two feet down or—you know."

He said, "Sure. When I was traveling around, we'd talk about them. Mine was where holdup men in the old days had buried a lot of silver . . . I'm still going to find it." He laughed. "It's up the head of Bear Creek Canyon, sure as hell. Wore out the knees of three pairs of levis when I was a kid, climbin' around there."

She said, "Yes. But you went out and got the stallion that was worth the fortune."

He thought. "You might say I had to. But you'd be smarter if you said I was lucky."

"How much jerky did you have left when you finally corralled Mulemouth?"

He laughed again. "Oh, it had been gone since a couple of days after I cut his trail."

The girl moved away from him, and he could see her face dimly in what light the single watch bulb at the other end of the stable gave. "You got more guts than anybody I ever knew."

In the night wind, his shoulder was cold where she'd moved away. "Maybe so," he said. "But they're a damn poor substitute for brains."

Her laughter startled Brownie, and the horse threw his head up, shoving the girl forward. Lon pulled her back to his shoulder . . . Three years ago Joan hadn't wanted to go to a party Tommy and Dot gave down at the ranger station for two girl cousins of Dot's who were seeing the West. He had driven one of the girls down the road for more beer and kissed her on the way back, but outside of that it had been a long time, with anybody except Joan. "This is the first time since—it happened—I've been happy," he said.

Again she was gone. "Take a look at Brownie's leg for me," she said. "He banged it in the trailer."

Lonnie opened the stall door and slipped in. She shut the door after him, and he was in the dark stall, the air warm and heavily loaded with horse and manure and oat hay. He patted Brownie's nose, slid a hand up and over the gelding's neck to hold him; Brownie wasn't wearing a bridle. The other hand slid down one front leg and then the other. "Cool and smooth," he said. "And he's got a good deep bed."

He slipped outside again and fished in his pockets for cigarettes while Vera Mae latched the door. As soon as he struck the match, a figure moved down the line. Vera Mae called, "It's all right, Slim," and the watchman didn't come near them. She said, "You're an awful damn fool, Lonnie. Mentioning your wife to me—just then."

28

He said, "I had it to do. You'd maybe forgotten I have two kids."

"And a lot of memories," she added.

"I don't know about that." Lonnie sucked on his cigarette, and then threw it down. "Maybe I'm not smart enough for that. I'm sure'n hell bullheaded, though . . ."

Vera Mae's voice had lost its life. "What happened to her?"

He sensed that it wasn't a question, that she didn't really want to know. But he said, "I worked Mulemouth a couple of hours a day, got him so I could saddle him, ride him around the breaking corral a little. Said I was going to take him out next morning . . . Joan slipped out early, and did it for me . . . A couple of weeks later, I was riding, and I found her saddle, with the cinch broke, up in the pine woods . . ."

"Threw her?"

"She got dragged a hundred yards before her foot came out of the stirrup. I was down in the meadow, where we night pasture the rest of the horses . . ."

"Good God," Vera Mae said. Her hand found his arm and slid down to his hand.

"Yeah," Lonnie said. "Yeah . . . well, for a while, I did what riding I had to while the kids were in school. But school's out soon. I had to see if horses scared 'em. Mike saw it, saw the end of it, and threw Junie down on the bed so she couldn't look out the window."

"Oh, good God," Vera Mae said again. "You poor kid . . . What would you have done if they'd cried at the rodeo?"

"Tommy Burns—he's district ranger up at Salal Flats—would give me a letter some place. I could work in a sawmill, I reckon. Or on one of the dairy farms down in the flat country. I can milk and plough and all . . ."

The other hand found him, and she was in his arms again. "I thought you were a rube when I first saw you." The words were a little muffled by his coat.

29

"I traveled rodeo for a year. I been around . . . Vera Mae, the kids are crazy about you, they never took to anyone so good, and—well—I'd been saving money in case I did have to move. Got enough to put in a bathroom now; there's a place off the back hall where I can knock a door through, and then I'll build a wooden floor, and Sears have got the complete outfits, toilet, water heater, tub and washstand— Unless you'd rather have a shower?"

She was shaking, and he thought she was crying. But when she raised her face, it was dry under his kiss and twisted up with laughing. She said, "Cowboy, is this a proposal or a plumbing catalog?"

"I told you I was dumb.

Her horse snorted and went to the other end of the stall at her voice. "Don't ever say that again. You hear me? Not ever again."

"All right," he said. "We'll make out fine, Vera Mae."

CHAPTER V

IT WASN'T EXACTLY a pickup, but they always called it that. Lon was glad Vera Mae hadn't laughed when she'd seen it. He went over all the things in his mind that he'd told her about the homestead, and decided she couldn't have expected him to have a real Ford or Chevvie pickup. Those trucks cost a couple of thousand dollars . . . A thirty-six Ford does fine, and if you saw down the rear end and build a good, hardwood body, you got as good a pickup as Henry ever made.

Sure, she knew he was poor, knew the ranch and the allotment together only ran a truckload of beef, knew the house—well, the cabin—had running water but no bathroom. Just a faucet in the kitchen . . . She'd understand about the grease stain in front of the porch where he'd drained the car last time, in order to get in the shade, and how the oil'd disappear in a little while.

Thank goodness, the kids were along and would insist on hopping out to open the gate. There wasn't any reason in the world he hadn't put the new catch on, except he never remembered to throw it in the car until he was almost to the gate, and it never seemed worthwhile to make a trip all the way down there when you had to go exactly there to get in and out.

Of course, with a forge standing right beside the house, he should have welded the leg for the stove, but it cooked just as well with two bricks under it, and for a man who'd bragged so about having running water, he should have put a washer in the faucet. And it was plain slovenly to have left the dishes in the sink yesterday morning, but they had had to get an early start or sleep two nights at the hotel.

Yeah, and before Duke brought Brownie up, he'd have to get the stall fixed where Belle and Betsy had kicked at each other and broken the partition down. But after all, the horses weren't in except when it rained, and the rain was over for the year. But if that was so, why was his slicker still hanging in the kitchen so you had to go sideways to get in and out, either that or get slapped in the face?

He wouldn't blame her if she turned right around and went back.

Vera Mae snapped him out of what was beginning to make the sunlight fade off this pretty piece of road under the Douglas firs, with a big stream running alongside. He said, "When these trees begin to give way to the pines, we'll be getting into our country."

Vera Mae said, "I'm looking forward to it," and he knew she meant it. She got up on her knees and peered through the window. "Both of them asleep," she said. "With their spurs on. Mike's left one has slipped down till it's on the bottom of his sneaker."

31

"Duke was sure nice," he said. "I'd never a thought of giving the kids wedding presents. Good of him to offer to bring Brownie up, too. Nicest thing he did was give you away, though. I had a market for you."

"You ole sweet thing," Vera Mae said. Her voice sounded so absent-minded he glanced over at her. She was still looking through the back glass, and he thought a cop must be following them until she said, "They're getting too much sun back there; they'll have headaches when they wake up. No, don't stop." She bent over and slipped off her boots. "If you stop, they'll wake up. Just slow down."

He had a hard time driving and watching her at the same time as she opened the door and slipped out. He cut his speed as low as it would go without bucking, or having to be shifted, and she worked back along the running board and jerked the tarp up on the bows with one hand, hanging on with the other. The wind caught the tarp and tried to take Vera Mae and tarp both off the car, but she was a lot stronger than you'd think, looking at her.

She tied enough of the tarp down to keep it from leaving, and started walking back to the door. He reached out to open it for her.

A car passed, the people in it—three of them, two women and a man—all wearing eyeglasses. The three sets of glasses looked foolish, turning to stare at Vera Mae; and when Lonnie looked back at her, she was obliging the tourists by standing on one leg, holding on to the door handle, the other leg straight up in the air, the tight hem of her saddle pants ending in a silk-stockinged foot.

Lon got to laughing, and the pickup wobbled back and forth a little, making the effect even better. The car disappeared around a bend, its out-of-state license bright and shiny in the sun.

Vera Mae collapsed on the seat, giggling. "The wild, wild West," she said. "I can stand on my hands on horseback, too. Both hands. Only I got to have a special saddle and a trained horse."

"Well, now," Lonnie said, "that ought to come in right handy around a ranch."

The creek went off at right angles to the highway, which began to fall. "We're on the east side now," Lonnie said. "See how the firs are thinning out, and the ponderosas startin' up." When she didn't answer, he said, "The ones with the red bark. Them and cedars and a few black oaks are all we have around our country.

"The underbrush," he said, "is mostly salal and some jack pine and white fir. It's not as thick as on this side. Boy, one time they took me to a fire over on the coast, and the brush was something! Grew right up under the trees and—"

"What are you nervous about, Lonnie?"

He didn't answer while they passed a big lumber truck bringing three ponderosa logs uphill. "Can't fool you, can I? Just going over in my mind all the things wrong with the ranch. A sagebrush quarter-section is kind of a mean thing; it don't make you enough money to live good, and it makes just enough to keep you there. You ever lived in a place didn't have plumbing?"

"You keep taking on about the plumbing," she said. "How often do you think I go to the can? I have fine kidneys."

Lonnie chuckled, but it made him uneasy to hear her talk that way. Joan had made him clean up his English, and he guessed Dot had done the same thing to Tommy, though maybe a man who went to college like Tommy had done didn't talk dirty in the first place. He hadn't, lately, known enough other girls to know how they talked when they knew you a little . . .

A lake appeared alongside the road, through the pines. He nodded at it. "Gettin' towards the desert," he said. "If we had a fast car, now, we'd be in our own hills in an hour."

They went through a lumber town, company-owned, company-built, out of company boards. The railroad tracks came up from the south and ran alongside them, and then a grain elevator, a cattle-loading yard, a big Quonset hut selling war surplus, a second-hand yard, and they were in town. Lonnie pulled into a gas station and stopped, and the kids woke up and hopped out, all in motion, Mike almost breaking his neck when he stepped on one of the spurs Duke had given the kids for "wedding presents."

Vera Mae got out, too, as Lonnie raised the hood of the car and put water in it. He told the man to fill it up with gas. Vera Mae gave each of the kids a nickel for the coke machine, and said to Lonnie, "I might as well use that thing. Might be my last experience."

Busy checking his tires, he looked up at her. "Aw, lay off, Vera Mae." But she winked at him with what looked like good humor, and took June around the filling station. He couldn't help thinking that he probably had the wife with the best figure within a couple of hundred miles; which was no reason for a man with two kids to get married. But he was sure glad he had.

They rolled out of town, and now it was tough rolling; ninety-seven miles of straight desert, with only a couple of houses in between, a roadside store, a state highway maintenance station. When he passed the latter, he said to Vera Mae, "Joe Howard told me once I can always get a job on the maintenance crew with the state. If we get short of cash."

She didn't seem to hear him, or didn't think he was worth answering. She said, "Is this the desert that's close to our place?"

He told her it was. And he got such a kick out of hearing her call it "ours" that the car clicked up ten miles before he remembered to worry about the radiator which he should have flushed out before starting on this trip . . .

"It's not so hot, today," he said. "You ought to cross here about the end of July. We try and wait for dark."

Vera Mae didn't answer at once. He looked over at her, and she was staring out the window the way he sometimes caught himself staring at her. He felt uneasy; try as hard as he could, there wasn't anything to hang onto, anything that would tell him what she was thinking about. Maybe she and her other husband lived on a desert once. Maybe she'd taken a trip on one of those fancy deserts down in Southern California, like Palm Springs or Twenty-nine Palms with her husband. Or with some other fellow. She was from Los Angeles . . .

That's what he mustn't ever do. Think about her with other men. She hadn't tried to fool him about what he was getting, just like she was getting a man with a cheap homestead and two kids.

Vera Mae must have felt him looking at her—it didn't take much looking to watch this straight road across the alkali flats—because she gave a little shiver, like she was cold, and turned around in the seat. "Is it all like this, Lonnie?"

He shook his head. "Road goes across the alkali flats," he said. "Where there used to be a lake. Still is, flood years. Get off ten, twelve miles, and there's buttes and peaks. Can't see them from the road; the high mountains kind of overshadow them . . . Look!"

He pointed, and then banged on the back window so the kids would look. A herd of antelope had gotten too close to the road, and now were retreating, frightened by the car. They turned and wheeled, like they had been practicing up, and then settled down to their steady, bounding run, alkali dust rising like smoke off a grass fire. The wind carried the dust ahead of them, and they disappeared as it settled.

"Ain't that something?" he asked. In the truck body Mike and June were jumping up and down and yelling.

But Vera Mae didn't seem to care much about antelopes. She had put on that faraway look again and was staring out at the cloud of dust into which the pronghorns

35

had disappeared, but they didn't seem to pleasure her. Finally, still looking dreamy, she said, "Lonnie?"

His hands were wet on the wheel. "Yeah?"

"Lonnie—that's where you found Mulemouth, isn't it? He nodded, and she went on, "And tracked him down, after your jerky'd given out, and on alkali water?"

He didn't know what all this meant. "Sure. Picked his tracks up just about this far south and stayed with him to the north rim."

"What a guy," Vera Mae said. Then she sat up, and her eyes focused on where she was. "Jesus Christ, what a guy you are!"

He felt fine. He stepped on the gas, and the old bus found another two, three miles of speed from some place. He felt wonderful. All the time she'd been daydreaming, she'd been thinking about him.

CHAPTER VI

SHE'D SEEN plenty of deserts in her life, this one wasn't as bad as the Mohave or the Colorado, or the Coachella where she and Kenny had taken first money for team-roping once. It wasn't as big, and she'd like to bet it didn't ever get as hot. But it was real, honest-to-God lonely. There weren't even signboards put up to tell you about air-conditioned motels and restaurants ahead. There wasn't a damn thing, after you passed that state highway place, except for a little board shack with a coke sign and a single gas pump. Probably these hicks hadn't even heard of ethyl gas . . .

Ahead, the tree-covered mountains came right down to the floor of the desert, and ten miles before you were in the town you could see it, on a little green shelf just above the desert, with mountains running right up on either side.

36

Ten miles wasn't long, even in this heap; they bumped into town over the railroad that must have used some other part of the desert to get across, and here they were.

Later on, maybe, she'd see something in this place where she planned to spend the rest of her life, but now it looked like any other hick town. Lonnie stopped the car in front of a chain store and went on in, telling her he had a couple of things to get. She didn't go along because the big lug had a grin that meant he was getting a surprise for her.

When he crossed the pavement no less than three lady shoppers turned to look after him. But he'd never know it. Not because he was a hick, but because he was that kind of guy.

He came back, put a cardboard box in the back with the kids, and climbed in, grinning. "Always get a few groceries here," he said. "The store up at Salal Flats is higher, and there's a lot they don't have." But he wouldn't tell her what he'd bought for her.

They ground on up out of town, most of the time having to go into second on the curves, and now it was all that thin-brushed red-bark pine that Lon had called—she couldn't remember, some kind of pine tree. Some of them had the lines on the bark running straight up and down instead of in blotches. She pointed. "That's a big pine, Lonnie."

"Doggone, sister, you're ignorant. That's a incense cedar. The ponderosas are the ones got that shaggy bark."

"Guess I'm just plain dumb, Lonnie. Only—does it make much difference? I mean, I don't need another merit badge."

He said, "Well—you make a fence post out of pine, and it'll rot. Or, say, you want to make a bridge, and your stringers are cedar, a truck'd break through."

Lonnie looked so solemn giving her this advice, she couldn't keep from laughing. Then, when he gave her the solemn owlish look he used sometimes—like a professor finding a new kind of bug—she laughed all the louder. Then he said one of those things that always made her end up feeling better inside than she had ever felt with anyone else.

"Well, Vera Mae, they's so damned many things you know I don't, I gotta show off once in a while, so you won't be ashamed of me."

She had promised herself she was going to be completely honest with this guy and see how it felt. She couldn't remember ever being that in her life before. "Ashamed of you? Brother! Lonnie, do you know when you went into the Safeway, three dames gave you the eye?"

"Aw, cut it out, Vera Mae, or I'll be gettin' red in the face. Never did meet such a gal for putting it on a fellow!" He raised a hand and pointed. "We're almost home."

Alongside the road was a big wooden sign, shield-shaped, and fancifully carved. It said, "Entering Bearclaw National Forest," and some more stuff too small for her to read in time. "Salal Flats is the first ranger district," he said. "Red Rock starts about five miles past our place."

Coming back from Fresno one time, she and Duke and Kenny and some of the gang had gone through Yosemite. She couldn't remember anybody living there; in fact they'd talked about good pasture going to waste . . .

"You mean we live in a park, Lonnie? How'd you work that?"

"Not a park," he said. "A national forest. It's different . . ."

She put on her party voice. "I know. Like pine and cedars."

He rewarded her with a laugh. "I'll get Tommy to tell you about it. He's the district ranger. We'll eat lunch at his house."

"Oh. Did you call him up from the store?"

Lon said, "Don't have to call him up. Old Tommy and I are real friends."

"Well, stop some place so I can fix up a little. I don't

38

want your friends to think you married something you found in a junk yard."

"Just the way you are," he said, "you're about as pretty as has ever come over the ridge. Maybe a little prettier."

The nice feeling came again, but there was a little fear. "Tommy married?"

"Sure," Lon said. "Married a gal named Dot, for Dorothy. They met in college, been married ever since. Fine gal. There ain't many college girls would put up with living up here; the last ranger we had, his wife ran away on him."

But it's good enough for me, all right. I'm not a college girl like Mrs. Dot for Dorothy. Who no doubt runs the local branch of the Ladies' Aid and Feminine Hygiene Society and—from the way Lonnie is shifting around on the seat—can decide once and for all if Lonnie can go on being married to me, or whether he has to throw me back like a fish. I sure hope I make out.

They topped a little ridge and slid down into a valley, and then Lon stopped the car where another sign like the first said, "Salal Flats Public Camp, Bearclaw National Forest." There was a big "U.S." in the center of the shield, and "Forest Service" under it. Back in the trees were some tables and rock stoves, it was real pretty.

"You can fix up here," Lonnie said. "There's a ladies' room and running water and all."

She heard herself saying, "So you think I better do something to myself before I'm good enough for your college friends!"

Then she was ashamed because he was drawling, "It was your idea, Vera Mae."

She reached over and kissed him, and said, "Why, honey, how wonderful, we've gotten past our first fight already." When he smiled, she felt all right again, but even so she combed her hair and washed the kids' faces and put on a new face and retied June's hair ribbon before she loaded back into the truck. This time she made June sit be-

39

tween them on the seat and Mike ride alone in the back. Somehow she figured it wasn't so important if Dot for Dorothy saw him after his new maw had let his face get dirty . . .

It certainly would be hard to get lost in this country. Here came another of those big signs, telling you that the Salal Flats Ranger Station was five hundred yards away, and damned if it wasn't.

Lon rattled the truck over a cattleguard, paying no attention to a sign that indicated that public parking was outside. Another sign said the office was to the left; he turned right and stopped alongside one of the uniformly tobacco-brown painted buildings; this one was a little larger than the rest, and there was civilian-looking porch furniture.

The kids jumped out almost before he had stopped and went streaking down a hill toward a big garage where some men were working around a red-painted fire engine —which Lonnie would probably bawl her out for calling a fire engine.

Her husband got out and waited for her to join him. Then they went up on the porch, and Lon knocked on the door, and again she got the idea that this was a kind of a ceremony.

A man's voice inside called out, "Come in," and before she could stop him, Lon opened the door and pushed her in, by her elbow.

A long-legged fellow about Lon's age was sprawled on the floor, fiddling with a radio that he'd taken out of its mahogany case. He looked up with one eye, and said, "Oh, Lon. Wondered where you'd been keep—" and then saw Vera Mae and jumped to his feet. He stood there, brushing dust off his green pants and khaki shirt; he also wore a green tie and a bronze badge like the big signs.

Lon stammered and stuttered something, but Vera Mae wasn't listening; the badge had made her react in a way she hated. Badges were worn by cops and deputies, by truant officers and fire inspectors, by guys at state borders who looked at you twice and suggested a little trip out behind the station; and when you turned them down got mean and made you take all the hay out of your trailer so they could inspect it for bugs. Badges were worn by guys who were respectful to people who had houses and regular salaries and money in the bank, but were hell on people who lived by traveling, who didn't pay taxes any place, who maybe separated the local marks from some of their money once in a while.

Badges were worn by guys who came and got Kenny in the middle of the night and would have taken you along on general principles if you hadn't—

Lonnie was saying, "Oh, hell, Tommy, what I'm trying to say is, Vera Mae is Mrs. Verdoux; we got married this morning!"

Tommy let out a whoop and yelled, "Dot!" Then he flung his long arms around Vera Mae and gave her a kiss on the cheek and a hug. She could feel his badge through her blouse. But this was Lonnie's friend.

He was still hanging on to her when a woman's voice said, "Well—Lonnie—"

Tommy took one long arm from around Vera Mae and swung around to face the kitchen door.

The girl who was standing there was taller than Vera Mae, and thinner; she was about as thin a girl as was necessary. Her short-sleeved khaki shirt didn't bulge, and her levi pants hardly did, either. She had black hair—one lock of which was hanging down over her eyes kind of damp—and no make-up on.

And she didn't take her eyes off her husband's arm around Vera Mae while Lon repeated that he was married, that this was his wife. Then she said, "Well, congratulations, both of you. I've got to see about the soup," and disappeared back through the swinging door.

The two men seemed to realize that they'd done things all wrong. She was almost sorry for them as they stood

41

there and looked at each other. Tommy said, "I was just trying to fix Dot's radio, Lon. Know anything about them?"

"Hardly at all," Lon said. "But I could hold things for you—"

Vera Mae forced back a laugh. They looked just like kids that had caught a nice mouse and given it to their teacher for a present. She said, "Maybe I can help with that soup," and as she started after Dot for Dorothy, saw their faces brighten. As her back turned, they sat down on the floor with the radio.

She burst into the kitchen saying, "Honey, I didn't mean to pop into you like—" but her hostess wasn't there. There was a pot of soup on the stove, all right; but no Dot stirring it. Idly, she lifted the lid of the pan and took the spoon off the drainboard to stir the brown liquid. Barley and celery and squares of carrots came swirling up, and the smell was lovely, and she realized that they hadn't eaten since six that morning, and that it was almost three now. She took a spoonful of the soup up, and it tasted as good as it smelled.

A current of air behind her told her she was being watched. She gulped the rest of the spoonful hurriedly and laid the spoon down on the drainboard. Dot was standing by the other door, watching her.

Vera Mae said, "I'm sorry. I came out here to apologize to you for bouncing in the way we did, and then the soup smelled so good—"

Dot's eyes were cool, but she said, "It doesn't matter." She picked up the spoon and tasted the soup herself, and then put the spoon down, not on the drainboard the way Vera Mae had done, but hanging over the edge to drip into the sink.

"You get the cheese out of the icebox and slice it," Dot said. "If you want to help."

"Of course," Vera Mae said.

Dot said, "I'm having soup and Waldorf salad and toasted cheese sandwiches."

42

"All right," Vera Mae said. "I'm not a great hand at cooking, but toasted cheese sandwiches I can manage. Doggone good thing you didn't tell me just to whip up a Waldorf salad."

Dot's hands were busy with a big knife at the breadboard, chopping up parsley. She slid the green dust on her knife and into the soup. "You'll have to learn," she said. "We always make the salads."

Vera Mae, being competent with packaged cheese and soft oleo and sliced bread, looked up. "We?"

Dot got a salad bowl out of the icebox, already filled with things. She started throwing in nuts and sliced apples. "The Forest Service gals always bring the salads to the PTA," she said. "The ladies from up at the hatchery make the cakes, and the independent girls bring all the rest of the junk. You know, Mother Trellis and the other ranchers, and Helen Clinto, though she really should be in with us, because Clint's Department of Agriculture, just like the Forest Service."

Vera Mae felt uncertain. But this was the wife of Lonnie's best friend, and she was being a lot nicer than Vera Mae would have been in the same circumstance. Least a girl could do was be nice right back at her. "Thanks for asking me to join your group, but I better stay with the independent gals till I get to cook better. Don't want to drag your reputation down."

"Oh, don't be silly," Dot said. "I'll show you how to make all kinds of salads. I feel kind of responsible, with Tommy the only regular forester on the district. Down at Firtree, where he was assistant, there were four of us, and the older wives wouldn't let me go around with the guards' wives, but thank God I never let that get started here. The ranger before Tommy was an old-timer, and they say his wife was a regular snob."

Vera Mae said, "I'd feel more at home with the ranchers' wives."

Dot had finished throwing peeled and cut-up apples into

43

her salad, was adding mayonnaise. From some place back in her childhood, Vera Mae suddenly remembered how you made homemade mayonnaise; Dot was using bought stuff. It made her feel better, but the look that Dot was giving her took that away at once.

"Well, I guess you could," Dot said. "After all, Lonnie does own that sagebrush quarter where he lives. But everybody's always thought of Lonnie as a Forest Service man. He's just about top guard, and if the stingy old Service ever gives Tommy any money, I'd bet Lon'd be the first man he put on permanently."

Vera Mae had never been known for her quiet temper. She got a grip on it with both hands, and said, "Lonnie and I are planning on ranching it, most of the time."

Dot said, "Oh, honey, it's not much of a place . . . Joan told me—"

Vera Mae said, "I don't know anything about Joan, except she had two damned nice kids, and a nice husband. And she's dead. But I know about the ranch, if I haven't seen it yet. I know we can make a living on it. And the way I know is, Lonnie told me."

Dot had forgotten the salad. "How long have you known Lonnie?"

"It doesn't matter," Vera Mae said.

"But it does," Dot said. "Lonnie's sweet, but he isn't a trained man. Tommy's an expert in land management, and he says—"

Vera Mae interrupted her. She felt awful tired. "Let's put the lunch on, Dot. I'm sorry I got into a fight with you, and you married to Lon's best friend."

"I can put the lunch on myself," Dot said. "Go talk to the men."

Vera Mae waited, but Dot didn't add, "It's the only thing you're good for." She wasn't that corny.

44

AT SALAL FLATS the country was covered with ponderosas and an occasional cedar. Then, as they climbed out of the flats, white pines began marching among their gaudier, coarser brothers; an occasional blue spruce intruded; and then the trees got smaller, and they went over a ridge, and the faint traces of the distant desert made themselves felt. The black oaks grew taller and the pines dominated less and less; salal gave way to manzanita, and an ambitious juniper had sprung up and tried to be a cedar. Then they fell some more, and as the trees thinned out to incidents and the sagebrush began to take over, Lonnie stopped, and the kids leaped out to open the gate.

It was a good gate, store-bought, of welded pipe and woven wire, and both the hinge post and the latch post were two-inch pipe, cemented into the ground. But it had been hanging ten years, Lon had bought it with his rodeo money, bitter against childhood recollections of wrestling with the homemade contraption variously called a gap, a Mormon gate, a Mexican gate and a great many more obscene and profane things. And in the course of that ten years, the store-bought gate had usually been treated with respect, but not always. Every so often someone in a hurry, or someone with a cranky motor and a dead battery, had driven through the gate; by pushing slowly with a car and then backing slowly into the open gate, a man does not have to leave the driver's seat. And it is a practice that, nine times out of ten, won't hurt the gate at all; if it does, it just bends the welded frame a fraction of an inch out of line.

So now the gate was bowed a little in the middle, like a line drawn by Einstein as against one drawn by Euclid;

which made the latch not quite hold—almost, but not quite. The two pieces were separated by about an inch.

The mail-order houses, in anticipation of this, make extra size latches, which bolt above the old ones and give a welded gate a few years more before its owner has to go through the tedious process of taking the gate down and beating it back to true.

Lon Verdoux, a diligent homesteader, had bought a replacement latch. But he'd never quite gotten around to putting it on. So Mike, with practiced ease, untwisted a piece of baling wire, June ran the gate open, the car went through. June ran the gate shut, and Mike retwisted the baling wire.

Lon looked at his new wife, but she didn't seem to have noticed. Next trip he made without her, he'd remember to bring along the new latch and the wrench.

The road climbed from the gate. Lonnie winced again as he shifted into low and went very slowly through a ditch he had dug in the last rain, and that would have taken him five minutes to fill. Things like that could break a spring. But Vera Mae didn't seem to notice.

She didn't notice, either—or maybe she thought it had just fallen there—a rock in the road that was a little too big for a man to move with his hands, but no work at all for a man who had remembered to throw a crowbar into the back of his pickup.

Then the road stopped climbing and wound down into the little valley that was all the deeded grass on the homestead—about eighty acres of it. It was a good big meadow, with a beaver dam making a little pond at one corner, a few black oaks dotting the grass, and a pair of huge cedars just behind the cabin; across the creek was a mixed woodlot with just about everything a man could want in the way of wood; alders and cottonwoods and sycamores, black oaks and red oaks and post oaks, cedars and firs, white and ponderosa pines all mixed in on the one little ridge.

It was a hell of a nice flat. If it had been four times

46

as big, it would have made a real ranch. But it and eighty acres of sagebrush was all he owned.

Lonnie glanced at Vera Mae. But if she thought it was too small, she didn't say anything.

The car went on across the field, bumping a little, but not too much, and in high gear. It curved, though in Lonnie's father's time the road went straight—and started a gully washing out that was just about healed up now and grassed over. That was on the good side, but since Vera Mae hadn't seen it when it was bad, she couldn't be expected to give him much credit.

Now the house rose up so you could see it plain. Lon had forgotten all about the corner where the sheet-iron roof had ripped loose and he had fastened it down with a catacorner two-by-four and some baling wire. Sure loomed up from here . . .

And—oh, doggone it—he'd left his car-greasing overalls hanging on the front porch again. And the carton of old tin cans he'd been meaning to cart to the dump—he'd forgotten to throw it in yesterday morning, and it sure made a nice front-porch ornament.

But the only cracked window had been neatly scotch-taped, and nobody could expect him to take a window down and drive to town with it until real sure enough warm weather set in. And if he hadn't repainted the new piece of siding that replaced one Bob had torn off with his teeth once, at least the siding was there, and in place.

Maybe, after all, if he'd been smart, he'd have called it a cabin, or even a shack in telling Vera Mae about it. Naming it a house probably built it up too high in her mind, and she'd never stay here when she saw it . . .

He stopped the car, gunned the motor to get the gas up into the cylinders, and killed it. Mike and June jumped down to put chocks under the wheels. "Stop back here," he explained, "so's to get a roll in case the battery goes dead. The kids and me'll carry your stuff—"

She wasn't listening to him. She was just staring through

the windshield. He might just as well start the old heap up again and take her down to where she could catch a bus—

"Is this ours?" she asked.

"It ain't the Governor's."

"My God," said Vera Mae, "but isn't it pretty?"

LIGHT WAS SHINING straight in her eyes. She tried putting her hand up, but the light came through the flesh, pink and annoying. Then she tried turning on the other side, and her fingers encountered a shoulder, a bony and masculine shoulder.

For just a moment she thought that she had gotten drunk and passed out and— Then she was blushing. You're married, Vera Mae, married to a guy named Lonnie Verdoux. A pretty wonderful guy. Married and settled down on a ranch. With two kids. Well, she knew what to do about all that. Married women, ranchers' wives, got up and got breakfast. They fed the chickens and they washed the kids' faces and—hell, she supposed they did a big washing after that.

She grabbed up her clothes. Dress in the bathroom, so as not to wake Lonnie. The poor guy looked deadbeat.

Grinning a little, she remembered there wasn't any bathroom; remembered Lonnie's speech about it. To him, the bathroom was as good as built, because he'd decided where it was going to go, and the funny part of it was, to her it was as good as built, too.

There might be a lot of things wrong with Lonnie Verdoux, and no doubt she'd find them out in time, because God never made a perfect man, but not doing what he promised to do wasn't one of them.

48

The outhouse was clean, smelling of chloride, and the water ran strong in the kitchen sink. She put on a kettle to boil. Like a movie where a doctor comes in; first thing to do is boil some water.

She fumbled around the cupboard and found coffee. But she couldn't find a drip pot or a percolator any place. Well, boiled coffee—there was an old-fashioned, huge coffeepot on the stove. When she picked it up, it was half-full. She lit the flame under it, strong and yellow.

The teakettle was hissing a little. Not boiling yet, but showing life. She poured some into a washbasin, doused her face and hands, worked on them.

Something butted at her, like a colt asking for grain. It was the little girl, June. Her head was bent forward, her eyes half-closed; the kid was still asleep, but moving around looking for something. The short arms went around her waist, the small face nuzzled into Vera Mae's flank, just above her bony hip.

Everything inside Vera Mae turned over, kind of wet-like. This was what women were meant for, maybe. It said so in movies and books. Nothing any man had ever done to her had made her feel as good as this. She put her hand between June's shoulder blades and wriggled the kid closer, then shoved her away a little, and raised the small face with one hand while the washrag erased sleep from blue eyes.

"Hey," she said. "When we wash, we wash clear back." There was a well-defined line of grime just forward of each ear, going under the chin and meeting at the V of June's collarbone. She unbuttoned the flannelette nightgown and policed up the chicken-thin chest and neck and ears.

"Can't say you went to bed dirty, but you weren't exactly clean." The kitchen was warm now. She pulled the nightgown over June's head and spanked her toward the chair where her clothes were piled. "Get dressed and go wake up your brother."

Struggling to get the dress over her head, June said in-

49

dignantly, "He always sleeps laster. Then he's dressed afore me."

"Be-fore," Vera Mae said automatically. "Sure, boys don't have hair to do. I got an idea for fixing yours different."

The small head emerged from the dress finally. "Vera Mae, I love you. What we got for breakfast?"

"Pancakes 'n' bacon."

June said, "I'll fix the milk." She got out a can of cow, and poured two glasses half-full, added water from the tap. As she set the glasses down on the table, her brother lurched into the room, already dressed and buttoning his shirt. He shot Vera Mae a grin, sat down, and at once decorated his face with a white mustache.

The smell of bacon and coffee was strong now. Boots were heard outside, and Lonnie came in, his hair slick with water, shaved, booted. "Been feeding the horses."

"I never heard you go out."

"You and June was so busy talkin' Paris fashions an' what not, you never heard an elephant."

He grinned, and all of a sudden she knew she'd been wrong before. She might have a couple of dozen kids of her own, and none of 'em could ever do to her what Lon could do, just by smiling. But she said, "Sit down, cowboy. Don't like my men pitching hay before they've had their coffee."

"That's the way I like to hear women talk—hey, Vera Mae. That's June's nightgown you're usin' for a potholder."

She started guiltily, laughing. Then she was dizzy, and it was hard to keep smiling. The hem of the little nightgown was covered with appliqué figures, cut out of some kind of linen; little horses and dogs, dolls and stars and a couple of ducks. Not a store job. The—the other woman had done that. In this very room, maybe, or out on the porch, or maybe in the bedroom—her bedroom . . . Sitting there, cutting out silly little figures to make a little girl laugh, and carefully sewing them on the hem of a little nightgown. Maybe next to the Aladdin lamp there, while Lon sat across, cleaning his boots or looking up stuff in the Sears catalog or—

God damn you!

She almost thought she'd said it out loud, but she guessed she hadn't, because Lon was still holding out his coffeecup, and the kids were still smiling at her with their eyes, waiting for their saddle-blanket cakes, and the sun was still shining outside.

"Here, June," she said, "go put this in your bedroom before I forget and mop the floor with it. Doggone an absent-minded woman."

She put flapjacks on all their plates, stood behind June, plaiting the thin hair neatly into four-strand flat plaits, then wrapping it into two buns, flat on either side of the round head. Lon was watching her, chewing as though he wasn't tasting the bacon and syrup and cake. "That isn't the way," he said. "She wears her hair—"

"This is a new way," Vera Mae said. "A lady likes to change once in a while." She was aware that she was talking flatly, without warmth; and so was he, so was Lon.

The kids sat there, looking from one to the other, their eyes big; this was a quarrel, they knew it like a horse knows when you're scared. Everything in her was dying to ask him if he liked it, to beg for his approval but she knew that wasn't the way.

He was a big man, a slow man. As long as she was married to him she'd have to remember that it was his home, he was the head of it; that was the way he was built, and only a fool would try and change him. To fight him would be to lose him. Not that he'd kick her out, or go hunt up a woman in town or like that. But he'd shut his heart to her . . .

Lon said slowly, "June's hair has always gone down her back, like."

She said, still keeping her voice harsh, "We'll try it that

way when I get tired of it this way. Or when June does." And what she meant to say was: Lon, I'll stay out of the man's side of this house—and brother, you'd better stay out of the woman's side.

Then he was grinning, and saying, "Well, doggone, if it isn't like havin' a new little gal. An' we couldn't have too many like you, huh, June?"

While June giggled delightedly and Mike went back to chewing down his breakfast, Vera Mae went all easy inside herself, wondering what she would have done, if she really would have packed up and asked to be driven out. But all she said was, "Michael Verdoux, don't wash your food down with milk. Chew it." The boy grinned back at her, recognizing her authority in a matter that was, after all, of primary importance to him.

CHAPTER IX

THEIR BREAKFASTS DOWN, the kids went scampering out. Lon explained that there was an old foot trail over the north ridge that they took down to the road where the school bus picked them up. He added, "If I had me a couple of days' use of a bulldozer, I could put the road there, save almost a mile to the highway." As he said it, he picked up the dishtowel and took up a position right next to her at the sink.

"Go on," she said. "You don't have to dry dishes in my house."

"I always—" he said, and stopped. "I'm used to it," he said. "Anyway I'm kind of counting on you to help me outside."

She stacked dishes and he dried them, and they were silent, the shadow of Joan strong in what had been her kitchen. Once or twice Lon started to say something, then shut his mouth and went on wiping silverware and glasses.

They finished, and Lon glanced at the battered alarm clock. "Seven-thirty," he said. "If that old thing's right." He fished a huge silver turnip out of his pocket. "Forgot to wind mine. What time you got, Vera Mae?"

"I don't have a watch. Forgot to take mine off, about a month ago, and wore it in a wild cow race—"

Lon looked at her. "You sure about that? Thought I saw your watch in the bedroom—"

Vera Mae broke out laughing. "Lon, you fool." But she went in the bedroom anyway. When she came back, she was carrying a little oblong box in her hands. "Lon Verdoux, where in the world?"

He made himself look as stupid as possible. "Well, honey, that Safeway store had a back entrance, and me bein' no better used to cities than I am, I found myself in the alley, and when I tried to get back, doggone if I wasn't in a jewelry store, and the man glarin' at me fit to skin my hide off. So I figured I had to buy something, and what's a better thing to have than something that'll make certain my meals'll be on time, 'cause, growing like I am, I sure get—"

She stopped him by putting her arms around his neck and kissing him as hard as she could. "Honey, it's beautiful. It's just the prettiest thing I ever owned!"

He said, "Hey, stop that, or I'll never get started on the day's work."

She said, "Brother, you've got a lot of days' work ahead of you. This one'll wait."

Later he put her saddle on Betsy, his own on Bob, and they rode the ranch. Turning left from the cabin, past the four box stalls he used to hold horses in when they were sick or when he wanted to use them in bad weather, he led her left, toward the beaver pond. They passed a structure like an old-fashioned fort, only without a roof.

Vera Mae said, "Is that where you kept Mulemouth?"

He nodded. "Might as well start takin' her down soon,"

53

he said. "There's a lot of good logs in there. Might build a—"

She interrupted him. "Hanging up your saddle, cowboy?" While he stared at her, she slipped from her saddle and led Betsy over to the corral. It was impressive. Eight-feet-long pine logs had been notched and hooked together to make a ten-sided pen; each log was a foot in diameter. The tenth side was a gate, swung between posts that were a good eighteen inches through. The gate was dutchdoored, so that its halves were not too heavy for a man to swing. Railroad spikes held them to the horizontals.

Vera Mae suddenly laughed. She put a hand on one of the posts. "Cedar." Then she laid a hand on one of the horizontals. "Ponderosa pine."

Lonnie chuckled. "Right the first time. Just the bottom layer is cedar. So's it won't rot. Can't have cedar too close to a horse, he'll eat into it. Almost as bad as redwood that way . . . Vera Mae, what was that about hanging up my saddle?"

She got back on Betsy and rode over till she could put a hand on his saddle horn. She took a package of cigarettes out of her pocket and offered him one; he struck a match on his thumbnail for both of them. "Well, you were talking about tearing down your breaking corral. You're thirty-one—Mike's ten. Seems to me, by the time you're too old to need a breaking corral, Mike'll be ready for one."

This was like this morning, Lonnie thought, when her eyes warned him to get out of the woman's side of their affairs, and leave it to her how June's hair was to be fixed. Now she was over on the men's side of the family. He dragged on his cigarette, liking the taste of the store-bought thing, not used to it—he'd been running it awful fine lately. "Hell, Vera Mae, a rider doesn't need a breaking corral like this for just any old cowpony. Just our regular corral, and a snubbing post." Idiotically, he added, "Best thing to make a snubbing post out of is black oak."

54

But it didn't work this time; she didn't even smile, more-over laugh.

She said, "Let's ride. I talk better moving—" and picked up her reins. He took her down to the beaver dam; he thought he heard a tail slap at their approach, but there wasn't even a V in the water to show her. But he pointed out the beaver houses, and the dam, and the marks of the sharp teeth on the willow stumps. "My dad used to trap 'em." He shrugged. "Now they're protected. State game men come in when they get too thick."

"Can you swim here?"

"When it ain't too cold—like now. Never heard of any-one getting beaver-bit." They both laughed, and things were getting better. "Mike and the Soil Conservation fel-low have been talking about planting willows, beaver-meat —up in the sage, where the creek rises. I dunno. Then they trap some beavers, move them up there, and keep them in, and they make a natural lake, and we put a siphon on it, and we're all millionaires."

Vera Mae was watching his face. He headed Bob out of there, and up the north ridge. She said, "But what's wrong with that?"

He was silent a moment, fooling with a burr in his horse's mane. "I dunno. Sounds like a damn farmer. After the first war my dad was rich, and he bought another half-section. Bought a plow, too. Then beef fell and wheat fell and only the Homestead Act kept them from taking this quarter away from him." He waved a hand. "Notice we got a piece of brush spurring down into the field? Didn't used to be here. Ploughin' grass land did that . . . It's going back. When I can, I haul manure and leaf mold, spread it on the brush."

She said, "But that's farming."

"It ain't breaking the soil," Lon said. His face got thin and gaunt. "I never had more than just CCC high school. I figure I'm smart to know one thing, and I don't want to get talked out of it. And that's, don't plough good grass."

55

Vera Mae laughed. "I'm not a plough salesman. Lonnie, Lonnie, you've got your own ranch to run. I wouldn'ta married you if you'd been a farmer."

He laughed, and the horses looked around as though they weren't used to the sound. "Well, I do some farming. Over here." He put Bob at a trot, swinging around into the brush, and she spurred up and came after him. She played with Betsy's mouth until the mare went into a hand lope. "Got a little project over here they call farming." He pulled up at a tiny valley in the brush. Little trees, each about two feet tall, stood in circles of scraped ground.

"Spruces," he said. "I got them from the state forestry."

"Your friend Tommy?"

He shook his head. "No, Tommy's U.S., not state. The idea is, you grow them for Christmas trees. You have to haul some water to them, come the very driest weather, and kind of hoe around them, but now they're beginning to drop needles, they keep the weeds back theirselves. Franklin D. himself put some in on his place for a cash crop, I read, in the book they gave me."

"They're cute," she said. "I never thought about anybody raising Christmas trees; I thought they just grew."

"You keep thinning them," he said. "You end up with a stand of big trees, ten, twenty years from now. Makes a windbreak just where the desert blows in, and it's good for the whole place."

She just sat in her saddle, looking at the baby spruces. He waited for her to ask some kind of a question, but she didn't. He started Bob up for the forest. They crossed the meadow, and when they reached the willow tree that was on the high point in the middle, they were in sight of the house again, and of the horse pasture down by the beaver pond; their third horse, Belle, saw them and whickered, and Bob and Betsy tried to turn home, and for a moment both of them were busy with reins and spurs.

56

Vera Mae said idly, "how come all your horses' names start with B?"

He said, "I dunno. We had Betsy first, and I never noticed. Belle's name was Hellcat, which didn't seem so good around the kids. Changed it after I traded for her."

"When was that?"

"When I was gentling old Mulemouth. Traded off a gelding I had for her . . . Figured to have at least two mares of my own, come spring. Now spring's going and I ain't got Mulemouth." He waved. "Here's the edge of our deeded land."

A little white- and blue-enameled sign, Government-neat, said it was the Boundary of a National Forest. "That thing won't stop a cow," Vera Mae said. "What happens if our stock wanders up here? The rangers shoot them?"

Lonnie said patiently, "We've got the right to graze sixteen cattle on the forest ten months in the year. That's where they are now."

"Pardon me for being dumb."

The land had gotten steeper, the trees closer together, their needles killing off any chance of grass, of anything but weeds and thin brush and sickly-looking seedlings. The trail had been made by cows, possibly following an old deer run; then, suddenly, it curved and met a ten-foot-wide dirt road heading up a canyon. Lonnie told her this was a truck trail. "Forest Service maintains it."

They rode the floor of the canyon, which rose and fell, but always climbed a little. The road was good, and Bob trotted while Betsy did her gentle lope. They came to a gate, locked, and Lonnie had a key and used it.

After the gate the canyon leveled off, mesalike, and some grass, already turning brown in the warm spring, showed up; cheat-bronc and Indian wheat, but grass. Once, rounding a curve, they scared a muledeer feeding, and he stared at them a moment before bounding away.

Lonnie pointed at a pine snag, rising black and ugly forty feet into the air. "Just last summer," he said. "Lightning hit her, and she took off good. Could have spread to the whole canyon."

"And I suppose Tommy came and put it out."

Lonnie looked at her. "Don't see why you get that look like you're spitting when you mention Tommy . . . Naw, I put her out. I was working up canyon with a crew, clearing water-breaks . . ."

The horses had gone ahead while they talked, had taken themselves around another curve. Here a geological trick of the canyon had made a little basin; a spring rose, there were a few feet of green grass around it, there was plenty of tall browning grass over the twenty acres of the basin.

White-faced steers raised their heads, their red sides shining, their eyes glowing, unafraid at the approach of the familiar horses. The horses, in turn, knew their business; they walked slowly and quietly, without snorting or bit-jangling. The steers went back to grazing.

Lonnie's rather twangy Western voice took on the Texan drawl that does—or is supposed to—soothe cattle. "They're about half-fat," he said. "Way I'm situated here, I can buy weanlings in the fall, when they're cheap, and they stay on the home place, gainin' some, during the winter. From now on, they'll really put on. They come out a good three hundred pounds heavier than I buy 'em, worst year we ever had."

Suddenly, he untied his rope and dragged it behind him in a slow loop, tossed it and dallied around the horn. Bob held steady as the steer put his head down and pulled back, and Lon took a bottle out of his saddle bag. While the cow still stood on his feet, he walked up and daubed bone remedy on a tiny cut.

Remounting, he rode in and loosened his rope. The white head came down, the red flanks heaved, and the steer thought about charging; Bob began to dance, face to the danger. Then the brute gave it up in favor of grass.

"Fly season starting," Lon said. "A little scratch like that could get blowed. Don't they handle nice, though?"

58

"Do they have names?" Vera Mae asked. She looked over the sixteen steers chewing grass in their tiny valley. "Wouldn't it be easier to teach 'em to come when they're called, and to lie down when they need doctoring?"

"Huh?" Lonnie was not a big enough fool not to know that something had riled her. But what it was went past him.

"I didn't know how few cows sixteen was," Vera Mae said. "I tightened my cinch real good and looked to my horse's shoes, we were going to ride our herd. We've ridden it, is that it?"

They had continued to ride uphill. Grass turned back into forest, and the horses hurried. Lon got down for another gate before he answered her. "Playing it safe, I turn off two and a half ton, five thousand pounds of beef a year. Good years, almost twice that. Present prices, that's a rough thousand dollars. If prices hold, I got my spread, too—and that'll be another forty dollars a head this year . . . No, you got it to know. It's half yours now. Say it ain't day wages. I'm living on my own land, doing what I can. Like the Christmas trees. Like hauling barn manure and topsoil into the sage. The way it's going, I got enough projects to add a cow a year, improving the ranch. There's quarter-sections'll carry five hundred, a thousand cows. Say ours'll never be that way, it's going to get better."

They had come out of the canyon, up on the ridge. He waved a hand. "This is all—down to creek bottom every way you look—this is all our allotment, given me by the Forest Service. Isn't anybody else allowed to graze a cow in here. Isn't anybody allowed to cut timber either, for another twenty years, and when they do I get first call. She makes a pretty nice spread. A man can ride free."

"That's the only good part of it," Vera Mae said. "That's what I married you for, and don't ever forget it."

Lonnie rolled a cigarette and handed her the sack. She shook her head and took out a tailormade, and he lit up, breaking the match. He stepped down, and when she did,

59

too, he loosened the cinches. They sat under a tree, the rough bark against their jackets, and held their reins.

"You'll have to pardon me," he said. "I am not too bright, and don't claim to be. I thought it over, riding home in the pickup. I was willing to get a sawmill job or a dairy job if the kids needed it. Way I feel about you, I'm willing to do it now, if it'd be better for you. This is a measly way of living."

"You old sweet thing," Vera Mae said. But she sounded absent-minded. "I wouldn't have you do that for the world. Do it myself first. But it doesn't sound like you make out. And cattle times are good."

"Sure," Lon said. "One year Dad did fine, and it came to a hundred and fifty dollars cash, for his whole year's cattle . . . I'm just bettin' cows'll hold up, a reasonable amount . . . Why, we wouldn't make out, but I got my summer money from the Forest Service. Comes to about two hundred a month for four and usually five months. Don't mean to brag, but I'm a good man, they put me on first, take me off last."

She sat away from the tree and turned toward him, supporting herself on one hand, holding her cigarette and reins in the other. "Yes, Dot said you'd worked as a ranger."

"Forest guard," Lon said. "Ranger's a pretty high-up kind of fellow. Most of 'em have been to college. Why? All the boys around here worked for the Forest Service one time or another. From the way he talked, your friend Duke did, too."

"We'll have to move down to the ranger station?"

Lon relaxed, laughing. "That all that's worrying you? Why, no. I'll work out from the ranch. Take a government pickup, and patrol eight hours a day, five days a week, or maybe a stakeside, with a crew in it, stringing phone wire . . . Except when there's a fire."

She said, "And then?"

He put a hand on her shoulder. The other one dug a little hole in the drying ground and put out his cigarette.

"When they's a fire, everybody goes, whether he's in the Forest Service or not . . . Look, honey . . . I got it to do. It's just about as much money as I make off the ranch."

A squirrel ran across the trail they'd mounted to come here; he stopped and fluffed his tail at them, but they didn't notice. A huge black-and-white magpie came down, and the squirrel disappeared in the thin brush, then mounted a pine and chattered. Lon took his hand off her shoulder and rolled his back against the tree, his legs sliding lower.

Finally she said, "Who would you have left the children with? School's out soon." She imitated his action with the cigarette, burying it in the same hole he had.

He spat in the hole and raked dirt into it with his fingers. His voice was dull. "I hadn't worked that out. I was pretty near the end of my rope."

She sat up abruptly. Her voice rose, and the squirrel jumped from the pine to an oak and then from tree to tree till he got away from there. "And I was a rodeo gal, going downhill, glad to jump at anything! You had to get you a wife, or lose your ranch! Isn't there a reservation around here where they'd sell you a squaw?"

He grabbed her shoulders and pulled her roughly away from the tree, pushed her flat to the pine needles. The blood rushed to his head till his hatband was unbearable, and he swept the hat away, to lie under the feet of the horses. His voice shook, and his hands seemed to be stretching for her throat.

In a voice he'd never used to her before, he said, "This is why I married you, and maybe the only damned reason," and ripped her blouse from its low neck to its belt line. The flying buttons frightened the magpie, which flew away, but the girl on the ground was laughing and the unheld horses didn't bolt.

PART TWO

THE FOREST

CHAPTER I

ALL OF A SUDDEN one day the air got restless; it was hard to settle down to serious business. Lonnie hung around the house doing little piddling jobs and whistling, and Vera Mae never got the dishes done till two hours after the kids had left to catch the school bus.

The whole countryside felt it, maybe, because that was the day they had their first visitors. Vera Mae had met them before, down at the Salal Flats store, Old Man Trellis and his son Stan.

It seemed they had a sow that had some pigs, and they wanted to sell the pigs off in a couple of weeks, when they were weaned. Stan gave Lonnie a copy of a government book showing what a great thing pigs were. The Old Man grunted something about the book not even being any good to feed the hog.

Stan was wearing a khaki shirt on which the tarnish marks of Army officers' bars were still visible; he was also wearing a pair of forest-green pants. "The old man is getting out of the pork business in a big way," he said.

The old man settled his horsehide jacket closer around his neck, though it was a warm day. "The ranch ain't big enough for me and a hog," he said. "The King Ranch in Texas wouldn't be big enough. The kid talked me into buying that sow. Dirty, gruntin', stinkin' creature that she is, her and her thirteen babies!"

Stan laughed. "There's good money in them," he said, "if you don't mind the smell. We about tripled our investment on the sow alone, and the pigs'll sell off for more than we paid for her."

"If we can find thirteen people crazy enough to buy 'em," the old brushwhicker growled.

Vera Mae poured the coffee that is part of all back-country visiting. "We could get bacon," she said. "And ham."

"All the four of you would want for a year," Stan said. "Lard. Headcheese, if you like it, which I don't. Spareribs. Sausage." His eyes were looking over Vera Mae and approving her. "I can tell you where to sell the bristles. The hide—"

His father ran a hand over his own bristles. "This is the way he talked me into it," he said. "He's always been like this. Oughta move into town and sell used cars. He's as hard to live with as a pig. Lissen, Lon, you got a right pretty wife here. Dresses up the back country. I was figuring on calling on her when you start patrollin' for the Forest Service. Buy a pig and she'll leave you before then. It'll ruin my summer." He stood up, put on his shapeless Stetson. "I'll run Stan outa here before he talks any more. Think it over and say no." And he stamped out to climb into the right front seat of a new Cadillac sedan. With a last look at Vera Mae, Stan had joined him and driven off, up the dirt road across the meadow.

"Who are those characters?" Vera Mae asked, laughing.

Lon shook his head. "Old Man Trellis? He owns just about as many cows as everybody else around here put together. Must have ten thousand acres deeded land, I dunno how much government grazing rights— Doggone, you ought to see the way they handle their cows. Cow needs roping, they drive right up to him with a pickup, lower the tailgate, a cowpony steps down, driver ropes the cow, fixes him, puts his horse back in the pickup, and off they go. Those horses never walk a foot they don't have to."

Vera Mae's laughter started up again. Lon was certainly glad to hear it. "What's a man like that doing, driving around peddling five-dollar pigs?"

Lonnie thought it over. "Why, he's got them to sell," he said. He suddenly had one of the thoughts that he himself had to admit were smart. "I imagine that's how he got all that rich. Five dollars is five bucks. We gonna get a pig, Vera Mae?"

She said, "Sure. Stan said they eat corn and garbage and acorns. We could probably raise some corn, there's enough land around here . . . My father used to grow some right in our backyard in L.A."

Lonnie said he didn't think it was the same kind of corn. "But I usually go shares with Mark Somers. He's got five acres on the highway with water, and nothing to work them with. Bob and Betsy'll pull a little old plough, and Mark and I usually raise some stuff together. Could make it an acre or two of corn."

"Then there's no reason we can't have the pig. Maybe two of them?"

He was the one who was laughing now. "You sound like somebody died and left you the prettiest diamond necklace in the world. You're sure a wonderful wife for a brush-monkey rancher. Sure. We'll figure how much he'll eat, and maybe get two." He thought a minute. "Hey, we can keep them in the old breaking corral, and—"

At once her face changed. He hadn't been able to figure it out yet, but something about old Mulemouth's corral made her face dry up every time it was mentioned. He'd tried to get her to mention it, to talk about it, but it hadn't worked. Times he'd tried, she'd gotten so she looked like Joan. Even the kids noticed it and got out of her way, and the kids sure weren't scared of her any other time.

He'd wanted a log to split and splice into the barn, where Bob had kicked a hole between two of the stalls. And instead of letting him pull one off the breaking corral, damn if she hadn't tied a boy's axe to her saddle and gone clear over the creek. Cut it herself, dragged it back on the end of a rope herself, and would have done the splitting and the carpentering herself if he'd let her.

64

"Okay," Lonnie said. "Pig'd be better off on the other side of the creek, anyway. Up in the wood lot. There's a little trickle of a spring up there I can run through a hollow log after I dig it out. Keep a tub full of water for him."

At once her face was soft again, and all lively. She liked planning things. "We'll build it three sides of logs," she said, "and the fourth side, boards. That way we can swing it open, and let him out—or her, Lonnie, do we want a lady or a gent?—to go rooting around in the acorns, like Stan said."

"That's it," Lonnie said. "Once a day we'll haul his garbage or corn or what-not up to him, and when he comes in for it, we shut the gate, leave him in there a while. Like Stan said."

"That way he'll never get wild," Vera Mae agreed. She sat down on the edge of the porch, her feet pretty close to the oil patch he'd worried about. She never seemed to have noticed it. She opened the government book Stan had left. "Duroc Jerseys, Hampshires, Poland Chinas—what kind is our pig?"

"Five-dollar pig," Lonnie said. "Get over to what does he eat and how much."

"Says here a pig doesn't have to smell, doesn't even like it," Vera Mae reported.

"Must be a lot of suffering pigs in the world then," Lonnie said. "Only maybe they never read the book."

"They eat," Vera Mae said, "pretty near anything. But a high protein content is necessary if the flesh is to be firm and— Let's go look for a place to put the pen."

"All right," Lonnie said. "Toss you to see who saddles up."

Vera Mae threw the paper-bound pamphlet at him, and he instinctively shied as it fluttered in his face. "What a gentleman! You're taking on that pig's manner before we ever get him," she said. "I'll saddle up if you'll sharpen the axes. We better take them along."

When she came back riding Betsy and leading Bob, he

65

tied the axes, hers short and single-bitted and sheathed in an old piece of fire hose, his double-bitted and with a heavy leather storemade sheath; tied them under their legs, though it was less than a quarter mile up to the woodlot, hardly worth riding at all, and certainly close enough to carry an axe in your hand.

"Horses won't stand easy if they don't get a workout," he explained.

She laughed, raising her knee up and down to see if the axe was comfortable under it. "How far is it to the edge of the desert? And how come you're so worthless, Lonnie?"

"Always get that way in the spring," he said. "Horses have it, too. From eatin' green grass."

"Doggone, I wondered what that was I cooked last night."

"It's only a couple of miles to where you can look out over the desert. I shoulda shown it to you sooner. It's kind of pretty. No, that's not the word—"

"Inspiring," she said. "Maybe you'll make up a poem to me."

"Me? I get all sweated up writing an order to Monkey Ward."

Lonnie had been right about the horses. They pranced across the meadow and then fought the bits as they were turned south, not liking the route. They felt different, like winter was really over, and she could tell that Lonnie felt different too; this knocking off work to go riding without even an apology wasn't like him.

As they started to leave the meadow to climb the high and stony ridge, they heard voices behind them. Mike and June were back from school and chasing each other up the footpaths from the bus stop, playing quarter horse; it looked like Mike was the horse; and it was June's turn to be calf, from the way they were looping around. Lonnie stood up in his stirrups and whooped, "Be back in a couple of hours," and Vera Mae's shriller voice added, "There's

66

cookies on the table!" The kids waved and went back to their game.

"Hope they remember to take off their school clothes before they climb on Belle."

"Mike'll make June change, and then he'll have to himself to set her a good example," Lonnie said. But he was still absent-minded, she could tell; but she couldn't tell the reason, and it worried her.

The trail went up a hogback through the sage. It wasn't a trail anybody had cut; it was just that up here the drainage and the rocky soil made it almost impossible for anything to grow, and the horses could pick their way without trouble. Once in a while dirt had collected in a rocky crack and a scrub oak had come up or a sumac, but you could ride around those, tramping down the crackling foot-high chaparral.

The wind blew from behind them, gently, insistently coming in from the southwest, a little damp; certainly this far inland there was no possible trace of the sea, but there was the feeling that the wind had come across damp and fertile soil since it left the ocean.

The hogback dipped and climbed, neither making altitude nor losing it; it meandered generally toward the south.

And now, suddenly, there was a dead calm, and the air was still, and a little ominous. Two magpies worrying a dead ground squirrel were the only things that moved; and then, as the horses pressed forward, their nervousness increasing, the breeze was in their faces, and they knew they had crossed a divide without noticing it.

There was nothing friendly in this new wind, though it was no stronger than the other; but it was dry, and if not hot it threatened heat—that and sterility. There was no more scrub oak, no more sumac, and cactus and yucca were coming up between the sage; this wasn't the desert, but it drained into the desert and paid homage to it.

Without thinking, Vera Mae remembered trips in Southern California where they had always clipped a canteen on each saddle; here, in this well-watered land, she had seen canteens in the barn, but never one in use.

"It dries our range," Lonnie said. "Sometimes it blows in from here for three days and more, and the grass just curls up and dies . . . And she's always up here, that up-draft, keepin' the rain clouds from piling up on our ridge. We get ten, fifteen inches less than they do at Salal Flats."

He cleared his throat and shifted in the saddle; Vera Mae found herself watching his face, he was going to say something important. "We gotta use every inch we get. You look at that beaver pond, and think she's a well-watered range, but that's just in our low-down corner, where it runs off; she's a sagebrush quarter-section, and no kidding about it." He stood up in the stirrups, and pointed. "There's your desert, Vera Mae."

Ahead of them, the shelf tilted up so gently you didn't notice you'd been riding uphill; but the shelf kept you from seeing the desert until you were right on it, made you think you were looking at just any horizon. Now they stood on the edge on the shelf, where the hogback broke off below them, a granite line of red in the yellow sandstone cliff, like the stain under a dripping, rusty faucet; and then the fall off, and then nothing.

Stretched for miles and miles—beyond count, beyond focus—was the desert; a floor beneath them of yellow sand and purple shadows, and all over were the buttes rising like monstrous layer cakes baked by an idiot. There was probably something growing on that floor, but the drop-off was fifteen hundred feet, and no brush or cactus or bunch grass could be seen from here.

"What's that?" Vera Mae asked. She pointed, and cleared her throat, ashamed at the feebleness of her tone. "Smoke? A fire? Or somebody ploughing?"

Under the brassy sun and the yellow-blue sky, a column walked—like smoke from a prairie fire, like dust from a tractor. "Dust devil," Lonnie said. "Like the waterspouts

68

in Mike's book, but dust. There's another, too far to see good."

"Good God," Vera Mae said. "You were kidding me about there being wild horses down there?"

Lonnie shook his head. "Lots of 'em. Antelope, too. Desert coyotes and foxes. See where it shines, below that second butte there? That's an alkali lake, dries up in summer . . . See there, something's moving. Could be horses, could be pronghorns."

"I can't see," Vera Mae said. "It's too far . . . Let's turn back."

"Sure," Lonnie said. "Deserts is for dudes—or prospectors. There's burros down there too, turned loose by the desert rats and bred up wild . . ."

They lifted their reins, and without other signal the two horses started trotting back to the ranch. When the wind made its shift again Vera Mae, for the first time in her life, could smell water. It smelled a little like pepper and more like chalk when they washed the blackboards in school . . .

By the time they passed the beaver pond, they were talking about the pig pen again; their ride, the view of the desert were forgotten, or at least not to be talked about just yet.

Then they came up out of the beaver dam hollow, and there was something on their meadow they'd not seen before; three horses, three people riding, and from the size and general feel, two of them were Mike and June. Lonnie stared, puzzled, sometimes people rode across the place, but he'd never known one of them to bring an extra horse along . . .

Then Vera Mae whooped and put old Betsy to the gallop; she went across the meadow toward the horses, and Vera Mae was yelling, "Duke! You old Duke!"

Lonnie, getting a little more altitude, saw a car and a trailer parked in front of the house, and grinned, the little mystery dissolved. Duke had brought Vera's horse, and

Mike or June was riding him; and Duke had also unloaded his own pony to stretch his legs.

Lonnie kicked Bob and let him run loose after Betsy; he was glad to see old Duke himself . . .

He caught up to them just as Vera Mae was making a wild Indian of herself, to the delight of the two kids; she had snatched Duke's hat off and was twisting Betsy all over the field, winding in and out between the kids and making the bronc rider chase her, his gray hair shining in the gentle sun.

Lonnie laughed at what a kid she was making of herself and sat back to watch the sport, gentling Bob's mouth because the horse wanted to get into the game.

And then he noticed for the first time that Bob was the only horse in the meadow. Duke was riding Lonnie's Belle, and Vera, of course, was on the Betsy mare; but Mike and June were riding mares, too, a couple of mares he'd never seen before, both sorrels.

CHAPTER II

THAT DUKE could ride; if you'd said anything about it he would have told you that he certainly should have learned something in return for straddling a saddle for thirty years. He ducked old Belle around and between the two sorrel mares, and rode Betsy—who was much the better horse—down and snatched his hat back. "Sure been quiet around the rodeo," he said. "Wrote the old lady I felt ten years younger, now that I'd gotten Vera Mae off my hands. Hiya, Lonnie?"

"Feeling no pain, Duke," Lonnie said. He kept his eyes on the sorrel mares. They looked young, five or six at the most, and it was hard to fault them, except the one June was riding was rope-burned on her near hind fetlock. June said, "Isn't she wonderful, Pop? I'm going to call her Sweetie."

"Your pop don't look too favorable," Duke said. "I kinda thought I got a good swap for old Brownie."

"Golly, yes," Lonnie said at once. "You're a horse-swapping fool."

"Matter of family argument," Vera Mae cut in. Lonnie could feel his face going slack with astonishment. "Lonnie wanted bays, to try for buckskin colts. Me, I wanted to try out what I hear, that you breed a sorrel mare and a buckskin stud, you got a good chance of palomino foals."

"I heard that," Duke said. "I never put it to the test myself."

Little June was wriggling around in Sweetie's saddle, making the horse dance some, but not much; she didn't fill the saddle, and her weight wasn't enough to be felt hardly. Lonnie said, "Which is the faster, Sweetie or—"

June was already off. Mike brought his rein ends down on the other mare hard, yelling. "Come on, Ruby!" and went racing after his sister.

Duke laughed. "Sweetie and Ruby," he said. "I ain't sure, but I think their names useta be Chiquita and Lady. But they're sure Sweetie and Ruby now."

The kids were racing in a wide circle. Mike was smart; he was keeping inside Sweetie, so that Ruby couldn't possibly help show more foot. They were about even, really; two good mares. But Brownie had been trick-trained and that to work with Vera Mae . . .

"Come on in for coffee," Vera Mae said. "No need to stay out here wearing out our pants. How come Turk didn't ride up with you?"

"Old Turk took off right after you did," Duke said. "Don't know where he went to. He's always been a little bronco. This is a nice place, Lonnie. Pretty."

"It suits me," Lonnie said. They pulled up in front of the house, and he stayed in the saddle while Duke and Vera Mae got down and gave him their reins. Out in the meadow, the two sorrel mares were sure getting unkinked; the kids were doing everything but jump them. "They're gonna wear those mares out before they learn their new names," Lonnie said, and led Betsy and Belle down to the gate by the horse pasture. He turned them out and left the saddles on the fence, and walked slowly back to the house.

He was puzzling over those mares. He'd learned by now that Vera Mae never did anything by accident; she talked wild and ran around like a kid sometimes, but none of it was what she didn't mean to do. She'd been fond of Brownie, he'd meant something to her, she'd made money on him; and he was a good roping horse, a lot more use on a ranch than Sweetie and Ruby—he grinned at the names—who had probably never had a rope thrown from their backs, or Duke couldn't have made the swap.

Maybe—and as the thought occurred to him he began to feel better—maybe Brownie was a present from Vera Mae's first husband, the Kenny she'd hardly ever mentioned. The one who went to prison . . . Sure. That was it. That was like Vera Mae; she wouldn't want to keep the horse, now she was remarried. He'd noticed she'd given away a lot of her stuff to the kids, some beads to June, a pair of real Nocona dress boots to Mike, and she'd done it quiet.

He began to hum as he walked faster. What he hummed was a song called, "All I do is hang my head and cry" that he liked to sing when he was happy.

Coffee smell filled the house as he came in. He hung his hat on the deer horn in the hall and turned right into the kitchen. Duke was sitting at the kitchen table, grinning over a cup of coffee and telling Vera Mae a story about some people Lonnie didn't know; Vera Mae was frying bacon and making toast.

Having figured out why Vera Mae told Duke to swap her good horse off, the subject was closed. Lonnie poured himself a cup and sat back, enjoying the story. When Duke paused to take a gulp, Vera Mae asked him if he'd like some bacon, too.

72

Lonnie shook his head no, and heard the rest of the yarn about how some of the boys had stolen a chicken and then gotten so fond of it, they couldn't kill and eat it. Duke finished and they all laughed, and Lonnie said, "You picked a nice time to drop by, Duke. The old lady had me out choosing a spot for me to build a pig pen in."

"We had hogs down on the Bill Williams river where I come from," Duke said. "I'll write you out my dad's cure for ham when I get back to my trunk. The best I ever ate . . . Yeah, they pay good and eat pleasant, does a pig. Don't ever let 'em get flooded, though. Can't swim worth a damn, their hoofs cut their throats . . . I'd like to see your stud, Lonnie. Vera Mae talked him up big when she was telling me to swap off old Brownie."

The big fork clattered at the stove as Vera Mae let go her grip of it for a minute. She picked it up again and flipped the bacon expertly. Lonnie watched her face. "He's down on the desert," she said. "We just came from there." All of which was true, but—

Lonnie had to back her up. He said, "Yeah. Been down there three months. It's a ways from here."

Duke was busy taking the plate Vera Mae gave him. Lonnie got a smile from her over Duke's bent head; she was pleased and glad and proud that he'd backed her up. Well, he'd had it to do; she was his wife. But he didn't feel good about any part of the whole thing. It wasn't like Vera Mae to brag they had something that they didn't have. And surer than hell, they didn't have Mulemouth, and hadn't had him when he met Vera Mae, and he'd made that plain to her.

Maybe there were people, smart people, city people or even rich back-country folks like Old Man Trellis who could put off thinking about something until evening or when they were alone. He'd never been able to rest easy till he got a thing puzzled out.

An awful lot of things were adding up. The way she wanted him to keep the breaking corral standing, though there was nothing to break. Swapping off her roping horse for a couple of mares who were good to breed, and that was about all. Asking about the desert when they drove across it—though she'd not been overcurious about anything else they'd passed—and wanting to see it the first time they'd really had time for a pleasure ride. Yeah. She wanted him to go get old Mulemouth back. Or she had wanted him to. Maybe now that she'd seen that desert she wouldn't be so favorable. It was getting late in the year to tamper around down there, even a dude could see that. And by the time fall came around—

Well, it couldn't be done. That was all . . .

The two new mares' hoofs were heard, and then the kids, squealing, and Vera Mae went to the window, very quick, the way she moved if anything might have threatened Mike or June. But it wasn't that, he could tell from the voices. "Company coming," Vera Mae said. "A green pickup."

"Forest Service?" Lonnie asked. His stomach tightened, and his feet got that funny hot feeling he'd always had during fire season when a green car came across the meadow. And three times out of four it had been a fire they wanted him for.

"I don't know," Vera Mae said. "Yes, I think so, it's got a big radio aerial."

It was too early in the year for a fire. Unless it was a plane crash—and they could be the worst of all, if it was in brush, because the gasoline—

Naw. Just Tommy coming visiting.

As soon as he convinced himself of that, he was real glad. The business about old Mulemouth had left a funny air in the kitchen.

Vera Mae said, "It's your friend Tommy and his wife. I'd better bake a cake."

Lonnie started to say that she hadn't time, and caught himself. She hadn't really meant it; she had meant she had better put on the dog. Duke started to get up, and

74

Lonnie pushed him down. "Don't go, Duke. Just some friends, the district ranger I work for. And his wife. They been good to me; the kids are crazy about them."

But this was said for Vera Mae, not for Duke. The old rider had gotten something wrong out of the air, he looked from one to the other of them, and the day wasn't much good any more. But Vera Mae said, "Don't go, Duke, please don't. I'd like them to meet one of my friends," and the way she said *my* made the day even worse.

Lon went out on the porch to welcome Tommy and Dot, and all of a sudden it seemed to him that there was something all mixed up between the way Vera Mae wanted Mulemouth back and the way she didn't like Tommy. His head began to hurt; he was sure getting mixed up. He looked at Tommy wistfully. In the old days he would have taken this to the ranger, let him put his educated head to it. Even the things about Joan, that he'd never told anybody else, wouldn't have told his brother if he'd had one, he had taken to Tommy, and old Tommy had filled his pipe and said, "Take your time and marshal your beef," and been a real help.

But this he couldn't share with his friend because part of it—maybe all of it, how could he tell?—was about Tommy and Dot and the fact that Vera Mae didn't like them.

Tommy got out of the left side of the car, and Dot out of the right. She said, "You still haven't fixed that gate latch, Lonnie."

"That's a fact," he said. "We haven't."

Dot laughed as though he'd said something smart. She waved a paper sack. "Wedding present," she said. "We thought the honeymoon was over, you'd like company." She slipped a bottle of liquor part way out of the sack, and Lonnie whistled at the green bonded stamp.

"C'mon in," he said. "Vera Mae's making coffee. we'll make it coffee royal. Friend of hers here, fellow who gave her away when we were married, Duke Holloway. And lookee yonder." He raised his arm to point across the field, where the kids were nearly knocking themselves and the new mares out, cavorting them to show their friends how well they rode. "Vera Mae's," he said. "She swapped off her trick rodeo horse for them."

Dot said at once, "They're certainly pretty things. Wonder if Vera Mae'd take me riding on them sometime?"

But Tommy stared out at them and shook his head. "Five horses is going to kind of strain that horse pasture of yours, Lonnie. Better figure on either renting some pasture or buying some hay." He took a notebook from his hip, a pencil from his pocket, and stood right there, figuring. Finally he tore out a sheet. "Comes to about four and a half tons," he said. "You don't need that many horses. Hay's high."

"Yeah," Lonnie said. "Maybe it'll be a damp summer, and the pasture'll hold up."

Tommy looked reproachful. "Take a chance on overgrazing, and it'll be ten years before your grass comes back. A horse is mighty clever about picking out the most desirable forage, too, and letting the annuals take over. Now—"

Dot wailed plaintively, "Got on a clean blouse, new pants, and a bottle of whisky under my arm, and you two are talking about grazing!"

The men laughed, and Lonnie stepped up on the porch and put his hand on the door knob to welcome them. But as he crossed the porch, Tommy saw the hog booklet fluttering neglected on the floor where it had fallen after Vera Mae had thrown it at Lonnie. Tommy lived by government books; they oughtn't to be treated that way.

When they stepped in, Tommy laid the little white book on the hall shelf, with some others Lonnie'd never finished reading. He didn't say anything.

Duke jumped to his feet when he saw Dot. Vera Mae was at the stove, sprinkling cold water in a fresh pot of coffee to make it settle, but she had changed into fresh clothes, a plaid silk shirt and clean riders instead of den-

76

ims. Had on clean dress boots, too, three-colored Mexicans she'd used in parades.

Dot handed Lonnie the bourbon bottle. He split the seal while he introduced Duke to the Burns, and then explained to Vera Mae that the jug was a wedding present. She passed coffee, and they all put whisky into it, and then she dug up some cookies she'd had hidden till after supper, and they all settled down in the little kitchen, their feet kind of tangled, but comfortable enough. Lonnie wondered if Tommy and Dot would notice that the sink faucet no longer leaked.

June and Mike came tumbling in, throwing their bridles down on the porch; must have left their saddles in the barn and ridden down to the pasture barebacked. He'd have to take the pickup down and get the other three saddles later, there was still dew this time of year . . .

He held his breath as June turned to fling herself on Dot's lap the way she always used to. But the little girl never made fool mistakes like her old man; instead, she stood midway in the floor and said, "Dot, you haven't seen me since Vera Mae fixed my hair over. Isn't it super?" They picked up that funny way of talking at school.

He watched Vera Mae's face and wished he was as smart as June. Well, if he couldn't be, it was nice to have smart kids . . . Duke said, "Think I'll take up a homestead here, Tommy. Down on the Tonto National Forest, when I worked there, the rangers didn't put out bonded bourbon."

"They don't here, either," Tommy said. The smell of the warm whisky was covering the kitchen, blanketing down the smell of horse on their clothes and of coal oil. "Except when their top guard goes out and brings home a pretty bride like Vera Mae. You used to be a guard on the Tonto, Duke?"

"Yeah. Two summers. During the CCC days. I was a patrolman one year and suppression foreman in a CCC camp the other. It was quite a forest; about six trees on the whole thing."

"I worked on a ranger district in Southern Cal where they said we had every tree named for a girl," Tommy said. "You know, Mary, Jane, Mabel. Brush forest."

"That was the Tonto all right," Duke said. "We were doing stream improvement between fires . . . I ain't been back there in fifteen years, almost."

The conversation died. Duke muttered something about having to go, that it wasn't his car and trailer. "Borrowed 'em from a fellow, didn't want to haul my six-horse truck up here."

"Better have another shot before you go," Lonnie said.

Vera Mae said, "One for the road, Duke."

Duke nodded. The kids had slipped outside again, nobody had noticed them go; Tommy and Dot and Vera Mae sat still while Lonnie got the coffee pot by shooting out one long arm and the whisky bottle by shooting out the other, and fixed Duke up. Light flashed in his smooth gray hair as he drank the cup empty in one swallow, and by that Lonnie knew that the afternoon was going; when the sun got level that way and came right across the kitchen, sundown was an hour off.

Duke stood up. Vera Mae said, "Excuse me," a little too politely to the Burns and went to the hall with Duke. Lonnie joined her, and they walked Duke out to his car; he and Lonnie put up the tailboard on the empty trailer. Duke took his hat off and turned it in his hands. "Vera Mae—"

Lonnie had one of those flashes that made him think he wasn't too dumb. He said, "I better get back in and entertain Tommy and Dot."

Vera Mae's hand was stronger on his arm than it had to be. "You'll stay here, Lonnie. I've known old Duke long enough to know when he has something to say. Say it in front of Lonnie, Duke."

Duke put his hat back on and tugged it over his eyes. "The old lady wrote me, Vera Mae. Said, come up here and tell you, you always got a home with us."

78

"Thanks," Vera Mae said. "You told me."

Lonnie felt the time had come to stick his two cents in. "No need to get sore. Mrs. Holloway said to tell you, he had to do it. Duke's a smart guy, he knows enough to be scared of his old lady."

"Sure," Duke said. "Sure. You know what the old lady thinks of you. Me, I don't share it. Too skinny for my taste."

"Spit it out," Vera Mae said.

"Well—" The hat came off again, and, like always, that made Duke look older. "I got to give her a report. You happy, or ain't you?"

"I'm happy," Vera Mae said.

Lonnie had a feeling this wasn't happening. People around here didn't talk to each other this way. Nor any place else he'd ever been. "Don't get sore at the man, Vera Mae."

"Well," Duke said. "That's it. You was always a good-time gal, Vera Mae, glad to see people. You seem happy, sure, but what's going on? Lonnie's boss in there, and his wife—"

"He's not Lonnie's boss," Vera Mae said. Her hand dropped away from Lonnie's arm. "Lonnie doesn't have a boss. This is his ranch, and he runs it."

"Forest Service pays me enough for the taxes and the groceries," Lonnie said. "Forest Service'll still be here if beef falls back to three dollars, like it did on my dad."

"Sure," Duke said. He looked out over the field. "And if you are turning over to horses, it's a slow thing."

He put the hat back on, walked a couple of steps. "Gotta be rolling," he said. "Excuse me for being a damned fool. Just an argument between a man and his wife, should he take a job or should he not, and old Duke had to stick his nose in."

He started for the car. Vera Mae reached out, and caught his high shoulder, and pulled him around. She had to stand on tiptoe, but she kissed Duke's leathery cheek, and Lonnie was glad she had.

They stood there watching the car drag the bumping horse trailer up the dirt road, leaving dust hang in the air. They saw Duke stop and wave to the kids, and then he went on, and over the rise, but they still waited till he came up the other side, and then the road turned and he was gone.

Lonnie felt wonderful, and he felt a little sad, too. He was enough like Duke himself to know what that cost the rider, and he didn't think he could have done it. It was about the hardest thing in the world to do to mix your tongue into another man's business.

That was the kind of wife Lonnie'd brought home; the kind that had friends like that.

CHAPTER III

BACK IN THE KITCHEN, Tommy and Dot looked like they didn't think their hosts had been gone too long; they looked relaxed and comfortable, with Tommy maybe a little glassy-eyed from too much bourbon in his coffee, and too little air in the kitchen. Vera Mae turned off the stove, Lonnie left the outside door open into the hall. "Gotta put up the screen door," he said. "Fly season's on."

"You can do it on your days off," Tommy said. "I figure on giving you Tuesday and Wednesday, like last year."

Dot began to laugh. "Like the tactful miner who told the lady her husband had been killed by asking her if she was the Widow Murphy . . . You were going to lead up to it gradually, Tommy."

"What the hell," the ranger said. "Lon's a big boy now.

He knows whether he wants to work for me this summer or not."

Lonnie rolled himself a cigarette. "This is kind of spontaneous," he said. "Doing what, Tommy? You haven't gone into fire season yet."

"No," Tommy said. "When we do, I'll want you to handle a trail crew . . . But right now, I got a lot of phone wire to put back up. Sleep at home."

"We could use the money," Lonnie said. "Vera Mae—"

She interrupted him. "No. Mr. Burns is right. You're a big boy now; you don't need a woman telling you what to do and what not to do. You're the head of this family."

"You see," Tommy said. "I told you it was that way every place but at our house, Dot." He and Dot laughed, and then stopped when the Verdoux didn't help them. Tommy sobered up, said, "Even so, Vera Mae—and would you mind calling me Tommy?—even so, if there's anything against Lon working for the Forest Service this year, I'd like to hear it. If for no other reason than that one of the things I get rated on is co-operation with forest users. Couldn't have you going around beefing about me."

"I'm no stool pigeon," Vera Mae said.

Lonnie saw Tommy look at him and quickly look away again; he guessed that he looked as mad as he felt. He said, "It'd be kind of good to climb a pole again, Tommy. Why, sure, I'd like to go back to work for you—and thanks."

Tommy nodded and reached in his pocket. He fished out a leather tobacco pouch and handed it over. "Can you pick out yours?"

"Scratched my initials on it," Lonnie said. He tumbled the pile of badges—just like Tommy's, but silver instead of bronze—out into his lap, and turned them over. "This one's that Whitney's," he said. "I remember the time once in fire camp when he burned it with a match to make it look like a brass badge."

81

"Whitney won't be back," Tommy said. "He's moved into town. Got a letter."

"I heard," Lonnie said. "Mark Somers told me." He picked out a badge and pinned it on his shirt pocket flap and then tucked the flap inside the pocket. "Got me a good pair of greens left, and some khaki shirts, but there's no sense putting on a uniform till fire season—where's my trail crew going to base?"

"I'll have to figure out which stations I can open when I see how much money I get. Then I'll put you and your crew up back of two stations we can't open."

"Leave Brush Creek and Bear Canyon closed, and I could work out of here," Lonnie said. He reached for the coffeepot. "She's cold. I'll heat it up."

"We've got to go," Dot said. "I've got a roast in the oven. Why don't you all get in your car and come down and help us eat it?"

"I've got dinner all planned," Vera Mae said. It was the first thing she'd said since she'd told Tommy she was no stool pigeon. "But you could wait and eat with us. We don't have a roast, but if macaroni and cheese'd hold you?"

Tommy said, "I could call Mark on the radio and tell him to turn the roast off."

"Some other time," Dot said, getting up. "And, Vera Mae, you just have to come down to the next PTA meeting."

"PTA?" Vera Mae asked. She went and got Tommy's hat for him out of the hall.

"Parent Teachers Association," Dot said. "Next meeting's Tuesday."

"I knew what it meant," Vera Mae said, "but—I didn't know you were a parent."

That sounded all right to Lonnie, but Dot took it worse than when Vera Mae said that about stool pigeons. "I'm not," Dot said after a minute. "We haven't any children. But there's so few women up here, anybody can join. Maybe I'll see you there."

82

Lonnie half-grinned and then swallowed it; Vera Mae had sure bought what she got. But he didn't think he'd tell her so.

It was almost dark outside. Lonnie said, "The kids'll probably run over to say good-by to you. Tell 'em to come on in."

Tommy said, "Sure. I'll put you on the payroll as of nine tomorrow. Get down any time in the morning. You can sign for your badge then."

Lonnie said, "Sure." There didn't seem to be anything more to say. Dot raised her hand, sort of waving good-by; a coal oil lamp went on in the kitchen, and he realized Vera Mae hadn't come out to say good-by. He stood there and watched the pickup bounce away, its headlights feeble in the gray light; the kids ran up from the pasture, and Tommy stopped.

Lonnie stuck his head into the hall. "I'm going down to get the saddles. Might be some dew tonight." Vera Mae was beating up the cheese sauce for the macaroni with a big fork; she sure seemed mad at that sauce, the workout she was giving it. She didn't answer him, so he went out to his pickup, just as the kids came up. Mike pulled the chock out from the rear wheel, and they both climbed in with him.

He coasted to start, and left the motor running down at the pasture gate; the hand brake wasn't much good, and he stayed in the truck, bearing down on the footbrake, while Mike got the saddles and threw them in the back. All five horses whickered at them as they drove away for the barn, Lonnie thinking how foolish it was not to build a little shack for a tackroom down there by the horse pasture. Maybe in the fall. With only two days a week off, a man couldn't get much building done during fire season. Two days off, and if you were a good man, lots of times you didn't get them, but instead were on a fire some place else in the region, making extra money.

But he didn't know any other way of getting ahead but

taking what work you could get, saving your money, putting a little into the ranch each year until she came to something. The water was there. Maybe a bank couldn't see it to loan on, but it was there, ready to be developed, and some day he'd have ten, twenty, even forty acres irrigated, and that was real money, even being as conservative as Tommy. That meant ten truckloads of cows instead of his present one truckload every year.

They dumped the saddles at the barn, drove the pickup up the pasture a way for a roll, and walked back to the house, a kid hanging on each of Lonnie's hands. As they came into the house, there was a hell of a lot of banging and clashing going on in the kitchen; Lonnie went in there, with the children for a bodyguard, and asked, "Are you cooking dinner or fighting it?"

Sometimes that worked, but it didn't this time. Vera Mae just went on pushing the pots and pans around. But she did look up and tell the children to go wash. They trotted off, and Lonnie started setting the table.

"Don't bother with that," she said. "I should think you'd be too good to set dishes. Just sit down and start polishing your badge."

Lonnie went on putting out salt and pepper, butter and bread. "Don't get in an uproar," he said. "This is just a job. Forty hours a week. During the war, it was forty-eight hours, and the rest of the time you had to stand by."

She said, "I said you were the head of the family, and I'm sticking to it. But—you knew I didn't want you to join the rangers."

"It's just a job," he said again. "And about the only one I could get and be home most of the time. Till the kids get out of school, you could go with me on the telephone patrol; it's kind of fun."

"It wouldn't be official," she said. "You might get court-martialed."

"Damn," he said. "You're being unreasonable."

Just then Mike and June came back in, Mike's hair

84

slicked flat with water, June's cheeks shining from washing at the outside tap. It was the first time Vera Mae had ever sent them outside after dark without a teakettle of hot water.

Vera Mae put the vegetable dish on the table. It was canned spinach, which Lonnie hated; he had known it would be. But she followed it up with good thick biscuits and milk gravy with plenty of salt and pepper in it; and the macaroni looked just right, nice and brown on top.

Then it looked like June, of all people, was going to smash it. She said, "Vera Mae, did Dot invite you to join the PTA?"

It was impossible for Vera Mae to talk mean to June, but she almost did it. She said, "Yeah, but—"

"Gee, that's swell," June said. "I bet they'll make you president, you're so pretty."

"Sure they will," Mike said. "There ain't any question about it, is there, Pop?"

"Not ain't," Vera Mae said softly. "Say isn't."

Lonnie had a hard time keeping his face straight.

CHAPTER IV

SUBENISH CANYON was on the Trellis place, alternate hunks of national forest and deeded land owned by Old Man Trellis. It was about eight miles long, and in places the floor was almost two miles wide; those places, naturally, Old Man Trellis owned in fee deed, by purchase, by homestead, by school section sale. In between these flats, the canyon would hump up and get rocky and make a natural rock barrier between one pasture and the next. These bumps were national forest, and along the peak of each the Government had built a fence.

Running up the center of the canyon, twisting with the

turns, was a Forest Service truck trail, a fire road; at each fence the trail went over a rail cattle guard. Going straighter, not following the easiest way, was a Forest Service phone wire that connected the Trellis Ranch with Salal Flats and Baldy Lookout Station and the spur that went to Brush Flats Guard Station.

Lonnie was working along this wire, putting the line back into fire season shape. Last fall he and Tommy and two kids had gone along here and unhooked it, laid it on the ground; Old Man Trellis's riders had previously driven the cows down out of Subenish Canyon to the front country winter pasture. The phone worked that way, most of the time; it only shorted in real bad rains. But now the snows had melted off, and the grass had gotten a good start, and Old Man Trellis was ready to turn five hundred head in here, to work up the canyon through the summer.

So the wire had to go back.

Lonnie was working on foot. He would get to each pole or tree, strap on a pair of long-shanked tree spurs, and climb to the insulator. He would wobble the insulator to make sure it was firm and hook a little pulley on it; then he would climb down again, tie the line to the telephone wire, haul it up, climb back up again, secure the wire to the insulator, and drop his pulley to the ground; climb down again, unstrap his climbers, and carry the outfit to the next pole.

The wire was only about fourteen feet high at its highest point, it wasn't really climbing like the power linemen did. But properly speaking, it was a two-man job. Only Tommy hadn't been given enough money for a second man; everybody but Lon and Mark Somers was out working truck trail, cutting brush and kicking rocks out of the way of the grader, which was making its annual visit to the district.

Lon was just as happy. He liked working by himself. He moved very quietly, wrapping his spurs in their leather straps between each move, and that way he got to see a

86

hell of a lot of wild life; deer, elk, a bear or two, and once a single, lonely buck antelope, strayed out of the desert country.

And, besides, it made him feel good to walk through these flats of luxurious grass, slowly curing on the stem, even if it wasn't his grass, didn't resemble in hardly any way his grass. For here, in Subenish Canyon, delayed grazing, undergrazing, check-damming, broadcasting, light harrowing had produced a stand of the purest perennials; grasses with deep, tough root systems that caught every needed drop of water, reproduced themselves from those roots, and left for the nourishing of the cattle all the seeds.

These little flats were cow heaven. Nature and the government experts and money had laid them out so the cows handled themselves; one man could work all the five hundred cows that summered here and have plenty of time left over for three more ranges like Subenish.

Lonnie's own grass, he thought, as he laid down his tools and slowly started strapping on his climbing spurs, was good grass. It was better than it had been when he gave up traveling ten years ago and came home; better than it had ever been in his father's time, it was almost as good as it was when the first white man saw it, before overgrazing and burning had driven it down.

He started up the pole. It was all right grass now, and could get even better. But, hooking up his pulleys, Lonnie knew that he would never—not in any way he could see—be rich enough to do all the damming, all the planting, all the irrigation he wanted on his own land, not to mention his government grant. And if he did, it would not turn out like this because he couldn't afford to run no cows for a year, or two years, while the new plantings got started.

Sure, Old Man Trellis got a lot of help from the Government. Drift fences and seed, engineering plans, cheap rental of Soil Conservation Service bulldozers. But he was a big taxpayer too, probably. And the soil deserved to belong to somebody who had enough money to treat it right, let it rest.

He leaned into the pole, and the spurs kicked out and let him slide down, his safety belt checking him. He fastened the long, snaky wire to the line and hauled up, secured the pulley line, climbed up and slipped the wire on top of the pulley, dropped the pulley, dropped himself, started unstrapping the climbers—

If a fellow could find a lost gold mine, or where some bandits or Indians had hidden old-time loot. Or maybe he could rent one of these Geiger counters and hit uranium; that was ten thousand dollars right off. No oil, but maybe—

He trudged through Old Man Trellis's grass, and there was a shining picture in the back of his head that he wouldn't look at. A picture of a buckskin stallion so big, so tough and so beautiful that his colts would sell as fast as you could raise them, so desirable that people would ship in mares from all over the state, at fifty or even a hundred dollars a mare—

Now, if a man on a job like this had a government book on rocks and could look as he worked along, maybe there was something like silver lying right on top of the ground, and no one had ever happened to see it—

He laid the kit down at the next pole and unwrapped the climbers. It was almost twelve o'clock. He took up his portable phone set, shoved the ground stake into the dirt, poured a little canteen water on it. He hooked up to the still down wire and cranked. Mark Somers' voice said, "Salal Flats," at once.

"About two miles up Subenish, Mark. You hear me okay?"

"Coming in clear, Lonnie . . . Time is eleven-fifty-five . . . Lonnie?"

"Yeah?"

"I told Tommy I'd pick you up this evening. We could get in some work at my place before full dark."

Lonnie cleared his throat. His hand was sweaty on the

instrument. Summer coming fast now. "Don't know, Mark. No way of telling the old lady I'll be late."

"I just saw her," Mark said. "She's across the road, at the PTA. I'll tell her. Or should I ask her, Lonnie?"

"Ha." Lonnie grinned affectionately. "Old Mark. Sounds like fire season already, with you wisecracking on the phone. Whyn't you ask us to supper at your house?"

Mark Somers laughed. "Some other night. I haven't washed a dish in a week. Unless Mrs. Verdoux needs practice."

"I wouldn't have a wife that felt motherly to dispatchers," Lonnie said.

Mark laughed again and felt it going too deep. He was going to cough. He said, "Got another call," and hung up.

Then he didn't cough after all. He sat staring at the building across the road, the building where the ladies—as they were always called—were meeting. It had been built as a Catholic mission to the Indians. When they had gone on the reservation, the priest had followed them, and the building had been, successively, a Mormon church, the first ranger station, a schoolhouse, and then an abandoned, glassless hulk where the young of Salal Flats—and some not so young—could dabble around in sex on a warm evening.

When the PTA suddenly thought the old building would make a meeting place, it came as no surprise to anyone that Old Man Trellis owned the land on which it stood. By that time he owned everything around there.

But he'd been very nice about the whole thing and had even sent Stan down to help the ladies put in the new glass and the linoleum rugs they'd bought. Afterward he only charged them a dollar a month rent . . .

Mark laughed again and took Stan Trellis's noon check on the phone. As he hung up, he saw Lonnie Verdoux's wife come out of the meeting hall, hesitate and then walk across the road toward him.

He opened the window. "Meeting over?"

Vera Mae Verdoux shook her head. "No. I walked out on it."

At once Mark felt sorry for her. But all he said was, "I know how it is."

"Bunch of old hens," she said. She stood there, lost in some misery of her own.

There wasn't much about misery Mark didn't know. He said, "I was talking to Lonnie, Mrs. Verdoux." It was nice to see her face light up when he mentioned her husband's name. Maybe she wasn't so deeply miserable after all. "He and I are going to break ground on the five acres tonight."

She said, "Oh." Then she asked, "The kids all right?"

Mark Somers stared at her. Finally he said. "Sure. I can hear them all down at the nine-car, Andy's looking after them." The PTA had a sort of playground down there, where you could park your children during meetings. "I said, I'm going to pick up Lon at five, go up and get your horses. I'll feed Lon here sometime."

"No," she said. "I'll go up now, bring the horses down, if you'll drive us home afterwards . . . I'll have to leave our pickup there, if I bring the horses down . . . I'll bring sandwiches and stuff, we'll picnic at your five acres. You and Lon and the kids and me."

"It seems a lot of trouble to put you to," the dispatcher said.

"We got to have vegetables," she said. "We're not rich people to keep buying cans."

"Yeah," Mark Somers said. "But I could feed Lonnie, I'm not much good with the plough."

"That's my job," Vera Mae said. "As long as I'm around, I'll see Lonnie gets fed. And the kids. If I have to pull the plough myself."

Their car was parked behind the office, where a roll could be gotten toward the creek behind the station. She ran toward it, got in, released the brake and stepped on the clutch. Then she remembered that she'd chocked the wheel, so she got out again. The car had rolled against the

90

chock, and it was hard to get it out, but she kicked with her heel, and it came loose.

The old Ford didn't have much compression; she'd left it in reverse, but with the hand brake off and the chock out, it started downhill, the motor coughing at having to turn backwards. But it went slow, and she got in, slammed the door, switched on the juice. When she put it in second, the motor fired at once.

She tore out of the yard at a clip that made the cattle guard rattle like a freight train.

From his office, where he was trying to figure a budget, Tommy called, "What was that, Mark?"

Mark Somers said slowly, "I'll be damned if I know."

CHAPTER V

ALL OF A SUDDEN, Vera Mae heard herself singing. Straddling Bob and leading Betsy, coming down the old, abandoned Verdoux Flat trail, she started singing, "Riding Old Paint, and Leading Old Ball." It was a natural enough thing to be singing; the truth of the matter was—and she was glad she was smart enough to know it on herself—she couldn't ride a horse and stay blue.

She hit the highway a half a mile up from the ranger station and put the horses to a trot. Half-kidding, she started loping them, to see how well they matched; and when she had them going nice, at an easy slow lope, she started gathering reins in her hands, and then, easy, stood up on the saddle, praying her boots wouldn't scratch the leather. Both horses should be barebacked for this, but—

As she went by the sign warning of the approach to the ranger station, she tentatively put her right foot over on Betsy's back. All this was wrong, it ought to be done in sneakers and with two barebacked horses and snaffle bits, but maybe so—

Betsy didn't mind, Bob didn't mind. She let her weight rest evenly on both legs and transferred all four reins to her left hand, throwing the right up in the traditional Roman rider's salute. She was going by the ranger's house now; she let out her shrillest "Ki-yi-yeeeeee!" and had the satisfaction of hearing a screen door slam in back as somebody—who else but Dot Burns?—popped out of the kitchen to see the parade.

The yelp startled the horses; Bob went down to a fast trot, Betsy picked up her lope, and it was no longer possible to ride Roman. She kicked back, knowing that she put a scratch on the saddle—but it was her saddle, won at Phoenix—and dropped straddling Bob's back, her knees coming in at just the right moment to break her fall.

She pulled to a stop in the public parking lot, tied the horses to the fence, as June came yelling around from the back of the office building. "I saw you, Vera Mae, I saw you! Jeeps, you were keen!"

"There's a coupla tricks left in the old gal yet," Vera Mae said. She swooped the little girl up—how fragile the bones seemed, how thin the flesh—set her on Bob, both legs on one side. Automatically she pushed the stray locks of hair out of the child's face; held up her handkerchief for June to spit on, removed a smudge from one faintly freckled cheekbone. "Have a good time, pardner?"

"Yeah, Mark went up to get Pop in the pickup and took Mike along, to Subenish Canyon. Said I could go but I wanted to wait for you."

"That's my pal. The office locked?"

June nodded. She was wise to almost all Forest Service procedure. "Tommy's taking calls over at his house. Mark left the door to his apartment open, he said, if we wanted anything, but he said not to go in the kitchen."

Vera Mae said, "Then that's where we'll go." She loosened Bob's cinch, lifted the saddle bags a little to let air under them, dropped them back down, and sedately went through the turnstile instead of vaulting the fence. She was already ashamed of rodeoing down the highway that way. As though walking out on that longhaired PTA bunch hadn't been bad enough for a day . . .

Mark's apartment was the back half of the office building; a kitchen, a bedroom, a bathroom. She saw at once why he hadn't wanted them to go into the kitchen; but there was hot water and soap and a chair for June to stand on while she dried and Vera Mae washed.

They were all done and mopping the floor by the time the pickup stopped outside the kitchen window. Vera Mae stuck her head out. "Hi, cowboy—"

Lon's grin was always a nice thing to see. "Hi, ploughgirl. Y'all ready to pull?"

"Pull, nothing. The horses pull, you push, and I come along behind you with a big whip."

Lonnie had gotten out of the pickup and come over to the windowsill. He suddenly reached up and grabbed her and hauled her through the window, while Mike whooped and June loyally hung on to Vera Mae's ankles and tried to hold her back.

"I've been asking for screens for three years," Mark Somers said calmly. "Maybe it's a good thing I didn't get them. I'll go down to the old barn and get the plough and the harness, Lonnie."

Lonnie gave one massive heave, and Vera Mae was through the window, her pants almost coming off as June grabbed at the cuffs. But, fortunately, June wasn't very strong; all that happened was Vera Mae's shirt tail came out.

She stood there tucking it in, straightening her hair, while Lonnie laughed at her. The pickup was coming back from the garage. Lon said, "I should have helped Mark with that plough. He oughtn't to lift things."

She stopped laughing, but she still felt fine. The heat of the late spring day had gone, the breeze that mussed her

93

hair was cool. "Mike probably helped him. That kid's going to be able to lick his papa in another year . . . What's the matter with Mark?"

"Belt broke in a mill he was working at. Slapped him across the belly. Broke his ribs, tore his guts loose."

She winced. "Poor guy. He get a pension?"

"Some insurance or something. That was what he bought this five acres with." The truck pulled up alongside them and stopped. The kids had been riding in the back. Lonnie said, "If Tommy catches you two riding with loose tools, he'll throw you off the station."

Vera Mae swallowed and said, "How about using a government truck for hauling Mark's plough?"

Mark Somers said dryly, "This is written off to Co-operation. I keep the books on this district. But let's get rolling. Who's going with me, and who on the horses?"

Vera Mae started to say that her saddle was already on Bob, then caught the looks on her family's faces. "Why, there's no saddle on Betsy," she said, "so I guess Mike and June'll have to steer her down there. You better take Bob, Lon, you haven't ridden him for two weeks."

Everybody looked so happy—including Mark—that she had to be happy herself. But she hated to pass up the chance to go for a ride—no matter how short—with Lon. Well, maybe on his day off, or lieu day, as the silly Forest Service called it. It seemed to her the cattle were about out of salt.

She got in next to Mark, and they started off slowly. As they turned down the road, Lon was already hoisting June up on Betsy's back; Mike was on the fence, climbing up without help, as he did everything.

Mark said, "Thanks for cleaning up my kitchen, Mrs. V."

"Why so formal, pal?" she snorted. "I'm the kind of a gal a man ought to feel at home with. If you don't believe me, wait till you get the returns from the PTA. Those dames have really got something to chew on for a while."

94

He was driving very slowly to keep the plough from sliding around. He put his arm out to wave a gas company tanker around him and yelled, "Hi, Johnny," at the driver. "You were a bad girl, Vera Mae?"

"Awful," she said seriously. She could see the mockery leave his thin face; she had a friend. "I don't know. I felt like I couldn't get my breath in there."

"I have an idea how it is," he said. "What'd you do, get whipsawed between the Fern Wentworth crowd and the Dot Burns crowd?"

"Whoa," she said. "You are talking about your boss's wife."

Mark said, "Well, no. I was clerk here before Tommy was ranger; I'll be here when he's transferred. You can say a lot of things about the Forest Service, but what they can't do is find dispatchers who'll run a ranger station for my salary . . . Years ago, they used to let the ranger's wife do it. Then for a while, they tried bringing schoolteachers out in the summertime and letting the ranger do his own book work in winter. But it's a funny thing, those college foresters are none of them good at bookkeeping."

Vera Mae said, "I feel like I've come back from a long ways away, Mark. You and I kind of talk alike. You ever work rodeo?"

The dispatcher laughed. "No. I get along with pretty near everyone—you know about me? I was a sawsetter, a pretty good job. I got hurt in the mill and had to switch over to timekeeping, pen pushing they call it. A fellow who can't get around well, like I couldn't for a long time, doesn't find many people to talk to in a lumber camp. I took to reading books. You do much of that?"

Vera Mae said, "Me? I don't have much time. But when I was traveling, sometimes I'd buy a *True Story* or a movie book to read in my room. I don't get it, Mark. What's the books got to do with anything?"

He said, "They remind you that this ranger district, our own little patch of back country, isn't the world . . . Why,

95

Dot and Fern—our two college gals, our leaders of local society—what else is there for them to do? They married the men they did, Tommy and George, because they loved them, I suppose."

"Or because they couldn't get anybody else. Especially Dot, with that figure of hers," Vera Mae said. Then she added quickly, "Meow, meow. I'm sorry."

"Well, in the normal course of events, those girls would have gone on living the way they were brought up—on a street ten feet from the next house on either side, in a town where a girl could choose her seven or eight close friends from among hundreds."

"I was born and brought up that way," Vera Mae said. "I got out of it as young as I could. It makes me want to throw up when I think of it."

"That's free choice," Mark said.

"So was theirs," Vera Mae answered. She craned around to see if her family was in sight, but the road curved. Mark pulled up a dirt road that went to a hole in the ground, partly walled-in cement. He stopped the truck and leaned on the wheel.

"My home," he said. "I pour a little cement, build a form, every so often. No hurry—why, Vera Mae, I wouldn't say those girls made a free choice. They didn't have enough experience to. For one thing, they'd never been in the back country except on a vacation, never seen it except as a carefree place, full of hunting and fishing and horseback rides—with the people you brought with you from the city. They didn't know enough to make a free choice, and I imagine both George and Tommy were sort of campus heroes—athletes, glamor boys. So that sex obscured their making a free choice, too."

"This went past me a long time ago," Vera Mae said. "Like Lonnie'd say, I'm a dumb country boy, and I know it. What's all this got to do with the way those other women fuss over Princess Dot and Countess Fern?"

"Why," Mark said, "that's simple. Tommy and George

96

are the heads of the two biggest projects up here, the Forest Service and the Hatchery. They give out more jobs than all the other employers put together."

"You mean those women are sucking around to get their husbands work?"

Mark opened the door on his side of the car and put his legs out, as though to stretch them. "What's bad about that? Up here—in all the back countries, on all the National Forests—we're dealing with submarginal land. Do you know what that means? The population drifts. They come up here, make a stab at it and drop out, go back to the city. You either have to be a millionaire, like Old Man Trellis, or take some kind of work from the Government or the state. If you try and fight it, you'll be going down the road, talking to yourself, in less than two years."

Vera Mae took out her cigarettes, offered the dispatcher one. He shook his head, but lit hers for her. She watched him break the match and drop it in the ashtray. "I guess that's why I blew my top today," she said. She swallowed a couple of times. "One of the women—that nice Indian woman, Mrs. Kaiser, I think—said Lonnie's ranch would never amount to anything. And Mrs. Clinto agreed with her. And then, all of a sudden, I thought that's why Fern Wentworth had been snooting at me, and Dot— What's the truth, Mark?"

He said, "I will take a cigarette after all. I smoke about five a week . . ." He made an act out of tapping the cigarette, lighting it, getting rid of the match. "I'm not a college-trained forester," he said. "Nor a soil conservationist. Ask Tommy. Ask Clint Clinto . . ."

"I'm asking you, Mark."

He said, "I've seen the reports. Both the FS and the SCS . . . So has Lonnie. I doubt if he read them all the way through, though they were about his own land. I'll be glad to get them— No, that's cowardly. Why, the truth is, Vera Mae, that quarter-section of Lonnie's has only realized half of it potential use. With care, it can be made twice as useful as it now is. With tree planting."

"Trees take twenty, thirty years," she said. "I'm talking cow. You mean if we work—and the Forest Service takes Lonnie on every summer—some day we can run thirty cows. Count them. Thirty. That's what you're saying?"

His mild face turned toward her. "Don't get mad about it— No, I know, you're not mad at me. Yes. That's exactly it. In ten years you can run thirty, maybe thirty-two cows. And that's your limit."

She puffed on her cigarette, she stared through the windshield. She had the feeling she was going to cry, but she fought it down. "There are ranches in the state that run several cows to the acre."

Mark shrugged. "They get a longer growing season. They have a different kind of soil. They're geologically placed to get more water. They don't have a desert backing them up."

Now she could hear the horses approaching, the saddles creaking, the hoofs clopping on the soft shoulder of the road. Lonnie was singing "The Cowboy's Lament" to the kids. He sang very badly. "And how about horses?"

"It's a business I don't know much about," Mark said. "Nor anybody else in the back country. Old Man Trellis raises a few head for his own use . . . I dunno . . . A good stallion costs a lot of money."

"But how about Mulemouth? The stud Lonnie had?"

Mark slid out of the car; the horses were almost there. "Why, everybody around here said you couldn't catch him —and if you could, he wouldn't be any good. Looks like they were right. He turned out a killer." He raised his voice. "You Lonnie! Hope you didn't get sweat in those saddle bags; Vera Mae packed our supper there."

Laughing, Lonnie slid off Bob while Vera Mae and Mark got the harness out of the pickup. "Old Mark," Lonnie said. "All the time thinking about his stomach."

Vera Mae slid the collar on Betsy's neck and turned it right side up. The mare was a little nervous; it was the time of year when all good mares should be mating.

IN THAT COUNTRY, spring turns to summer while you sleep; a man goes to bed with a couple of blankets over him, and turns over gingerly to warm the sheets; then, in the morning, he wakes up to find the blankets on the floor, and his legs bathed in sweat.

Out on the range, the grass was green yesterday, and growing like mad; today there is a brown tinge to it, and its growing days are over. But the vegetables and the corn on the irrigated patches—like Mark Somers' five acres— glory in the heat; the reverse of human beings, they need cold, damp feet and hot dry heads to do well. The health of the vegetables and the death of the grass make a bad combination for a farmer who has a Forest Service job as well.

School ended, and Lon went out with his high school kids; they camped about ten miles north of the ranch, set up a portable phone and an FM radio, and did their own cooking in a carefully cleared circle in the drying pine needles. They were at a crossroads in the truck trail system, and there was at least a month's work that could be done from that camp, working up to five miles in each of the four directions.

Because of the Civil Service ruling that a forest officer could work only forty hours a week except in emergencies, Lon got to come home two nights a week, while Andy Anderson, the assistant ranger, or Frank Knox, the relief guard, went up to the camp and supervised the boys. But the work was rough; his forty hours included only time on the trail, but before and after that there were cooking and camp cleaning, wood cutting and dishwashing. The kids did what they were told to do, and no more; Lon had to supervise them, and he did the cooking himself. Most nights he did a little tool grinding, too; injuries come from dull tools, not sharp ones.

Andy was a good man, and Frank wasn't bad; but it was Lon's camp. He worried about what he would find after his weekly lieu days of Tuesday and Wednesday, and he was usually right; the camp in a mess, a kid laid up with foot blisters, another one with a cold.

And all the time he was ridden with a sense of shame, he felt guilty. He could not tell Vera Mae that being home with her, working around the ranch didn't satisfy him; that he wanted to talk about the spike camp, wanted to run up there and remind the kids to do their work well, to do it in safety. Once he got back, and they had trimmed a trail much too low. Men riding in the back of a stakeside, going to a fire at night, would have had their hats knocked off, a tall man could have lost an eye on some of the branches they left; he made them do it over again, but he felt it was his fault for having taken his days off.

It had been the same for a lot of years; since he'd come back from traveling around. From the time the Forest Service let him out in the fall till summer his interest in it would fall off; toward April, he'd have trouble listening when a ranger or some other permanent hand would want to tell him about the woes of the district.

And then, even after he'd put the green tie back on, it was just a job; do it and get back to the ranch, which is your real work. But day by day, the Forest Service and forestry, fire-fighting, fire prevention, presuppression, would get more and more of a grip on him.

If there'd been a longer fire season in that country, the ranch sure would have suffered.

But the ranch got along; there wasn't much to do in early summer. The cows were up in the forest, and Betsy

100

and Belle were at the ranger station; Tommy had pulled off a miracle, he had gotten the supervisor to buy some hay and keep the two mares at the station for Stan Trellis to use on patrol once in a while. It took the burden off Lonnie's horse pasture. On his days off, he trucked garbage up from the station to the pigs; they had bought two of them, and Lonnie had acted before any other pig buyers thought of it, and arranged to truck the garbage away from both lunchrooms on the boulevard, two guard stations, and the ranger station. The pigs were growing fast, ranging after mast five days in the week, gorging on garbage the rest of the time; Lonnie was not going to have his wife truck swill.

With a salary assured, he took his savings and sent off for the mail-order bathroom; the mail-order house took a deposit, and rented him a set of tools to put it together.

He had a month's use of the tools; eight full days—except for the garbage hauling and the vegetable plot. Those vegetables were a headache; the warm weather and the irrigation made the weeds grow like mad—tough Bermuda grass and Johnson grass that some cattlemen had imported to the country, mallow weed and plantain. Mike and June each had a hoe, and so did Vera Mae, but five acres is a lot of plot, and Vera Mae, good horsewoman as she was, couldn't seem to get the hang of the one-horse cultivator. Still, the corn was growing. Mark was to get a ham and a side of bacon for his share of it.

This was in early summer, but early summer passed into full fire season as quickly as spring had gone into summer. The difference was this: in early summer, the desert wind —devil wind, they called it around there—would blow in three-day stretches. Then the desert would blow itself out, and the pressure would fall, and the damper west wind would come back and bring the humidity up to thirty and better; not really fire weather. So that any fire that started— and a couple did, from trucks backfiring—was an over-night affair; the men would flank it, the fire would blow back on itself just before dawn, they'd put it out and leave a man or so to patrol.

Then they knew their fire season had started. Lonnie—it was a lieu day—went to bed one night, listening to the trees crackle over the ranch cabin, and said, "This is the third day. The devil's wind blowing itself out—" But the days had become increasingly longer than the nights; the desert didn't cool off as it had been doing. The desert blow went into a second cycle of aridity, and Lonnie went back to his trail camp warning Vera Mae and Mark to use plenty of water on the vegetables; the devil was sucking it out. The wind was in its eighth day when he pulled on his suntans and pinned his badge on and knotted his green tie to return to duty the second time. He warned Vera Mae, this time, to be sure and put damp sacks over the wet cement in the roughed-in, unroofed bathroom; cement would craze in this dry air if it wasn't carefully damped down.

For nine days the dry wind ripped across the ponderosas and the brush and the rocks of the back country; everyone's hair was full of electricity, and so was the wind. The alkali lakes gave up their moisture in piling thunderheads, and suddenly the sky darkened as a thunderhead started walking across the forest.

Lonnie was just bedding down his crew when the call came. Lightning was on the Red Rock district, just north; the boys were to stand by with all their clothes on except boots—

They went out at four in the morning; they hadn't had any sleep to amount to anything. They went down the trail at a good walk, carrying axes and McLeods and two two-man saws; the strawboss carried the radio. They dropped off the trail to make an easy trip to a tree that had been struck; felled the tree, cut off the burning section, and left it in the center of a thirty-foot clearing, with a boy to watch it.

By now they were chasing the storm; they handled an-

102

other strike two miles on, but there was nothing to do there, the thunderhead had sprinkled enough rain to undo its own damage; Lonnie felt the burn with his hands and called it officially out.

Dawn was two hours old when they hit what might be called a fire; a struck hollow snag, shooting sparks up its chimney-like trunk. The fire already had run an acre when they got there, and they settled down to a nasty job.

They flanked the acre, and they cut a trail two feet wide, half in the burn and half out; the day was building, and the sweat poured out of them. Lonnie sat them down to eat K-rations before they tackled felling the snag itself.

The devil wind, in its last day—they hoped—still blew. As they were throwing away the empty K-ration cartons, Lon saw smoke a hundred yards outside his burn; they started cutting a trail through the heavy manzanita to the spot fire when another one sprang up behind them; Lonnie split his crew into two halves, and radioed Mark Somers for help.

CHAPTER VII

A WEEK LATER Vera Mae was waked up by head-lights coming across the meadow, dancing on the windows of the bedroom. She slid out of bed at once and fumbled around for boots and a bathrobe; she didn't own any slippers. It was cold tonight and a little damp—there might even be dew.

By the time she reached the front porch, the car had pulled sidewise to the house, as though ready to leave, and she could see that it was a government pickup. Then a man got out of the right side of the cab and started toward her; the truck went into gear and bounced back toward the gate.

Lonnie came up on the porch, and threw his war bag and bedroll down. He stood over her, swaying; he had an old leather jacket on over his shirt, and he reeked of smoke, sweat—and liquor. "Let's go to bed, babe."

She'd never seen him drunk before. Against her will she shrank back, afraid. Then she said, "Want a cup of coffee?"

"Good deal," Lonnie said. "I'm plastered. I'm stinkin'. Been to hell an' gone . . . Baby, we're rich. I run up fourteen days of overtime in a week."

He followed her into the kitchen. She struck a match and got a lamp working, pushed Lonnie away when he broke three matches trying to light the burner under the coffeepot. "Boy, you really are high."

He dropped into a chair, put his elbows on the table. "You're not mad, are ya?"

She said, "No. Of course not . . . Coffee coming up, Lonnie. Where did you get the skinful?"

He laughed, a little vaguely. "Tommy and I got old Schaefer to drive. We bought a jug, at the airport . . ."

"Airport? Where have you been, anyway? I thought you were up at a fire on Deadman Ridge?"

"Left there three days ago," Lonnie said. "They flew a bunch of us south, and clear over to the coast. C-47's. Had a big fire over there. Flew us back tonight. Don't have to work tomorrow, lieu day."

He accepted the coffee from her, gulped it down. "Whoosh. Hot!" He shook his head. "Gawd. Don't like being drunk."

Vera Mae said, "You aren't. You're just tired. When did you go to bed last?"

"Bed? What's that? Told you I been to a fire, two fires. I slept some on the plane. But those bucket seats—" He shrugged. "We was too crowded to stretch out our bedrolls. Ship was bumping all over the place, anyway."

He ran his hand over his face; the coal-oil lamps and the stove were making the kitchen unbearably hot. Vera Mae

104

got up and stood behind him, tugging at the old leather jacket; its back was covered with spark holes. Lonnie let her take it off.

"How about lying down on our bed?" she asked. "I'll give you a sponge bath."

He nodded. "You're a kind of a wife any guy'd come home to," he said. "From a fire . . ." He shook his head. "Run up fourteen days of overtime in a week. Four for working sixteen hours a day on my lieu days, two for working right through one day, rest for just workin' . . . Oh, Gawd, Vera Mae, my feet are killing me."

She got him to the bed, where he promptly went to sleep. His strapped-on boots came off easily, but his smoky Chino pants gave her trouble. By rocking him back and forth, she got him undressed, and bathed him with warm water from the teakettle in the kitchen. He didn't wake up . . .

She was fixing breakfast for the kids when he came into the kitchen, wearing blue jeans and an old cotton shirt; his feet were covered with heavy wool socks and no boots. June and Mike jumped up from the table to cover his face with kisses and pancake syrup. He picked them both up, each sitting on the crook of his arm, while he laughed at them. "Made enough noise comin' in last night to wake the beavers. How come you didn't hear me?"

"You weren't so noisy," Vera Mae said. "You didn't even sing any songs."

He laughed. "Had about three drinks ridin' in the pick-up. They just hit me."

"Like a sledge hammer," she said. "What do you expect when you don't sleep for a week?"

"I was on night shift when I wasn't on double shift," he said, "and it was too hot to sleep in the daytime. They oughta rig tents or awnings or something for us; that sun was a scorcher." He looked down at his feet. "Many thanks for the bath. I kinda toasted my feet."

"I didn't notice," Vera Mae said. She flipped fresh pancakes onto the children's plates, added bacon to the platter.

"The soles," Lonnie said. "I'll put borax in my boots when I put my boots on. Wonder if anybody minds if I collect the garbage in my stocking feet? It ought to be piling up, and me missing last week . . . Tommy said the weather report was for higher humidity . . . I oughta get a lot done today and tomorrow."

Vera Mae looked at him across the two young heads, Mike's still wet from his morning combing, June's braided and combed, brushed and shining. "You had about two hours' sleep."

"Well, I ain't a bear," he said, "and if I was, this ain't no hollow log."

He sat down and helped himself to bacon. Vera Mae put pancakes on his plate, and he tore in. With his mouth full, he said, "How are the hogs?"

"I saw them in the woods yesterday," June said. "Henry woofled at me, but Henrietta ran away."

"If I'd been there," Mike said, "I would have woofled right back."

Lonnie washed a mouthful down with black coffee and laughed. "Don't you go scaring our pigs now," he said, "or they'll never fat up. Who's going to ride with the garbage man today?" He loaded his fork, held it to let the syrup run off, and then put it down again, surprised because nobody had answered him. He looked around.

Vera Mae said, "Lonnie—I hate to do this—but the car isn't running."

He said, "The hell you say," and transferred the pancakes to his mouth. He shoved a piece of bacon in on top, and added, "Then I'll have to fix it. What broke?"

"Low gear's stripped," Vera Mae said, "I think."

Lonnie nodded. "Sounds reasonable. There was some teeth out already." He thought a minute. "Any juice left in the welder, Mike?"

Mike looked as grave as a man can with his mouth full of pancake. "Yeah. Last job we did was fix the foot of the

106

stove, and there was plenty pressure left when we finished."

Lonnie looked at Mike with such pride that Vera Mae almost cried with pleasure. "We're all set then, Mike," Lonnie said. "Get a good load of grub under your belt, and we'll do a day's work . . ."

But it was noon before they got the housing off the gears and carried the stripped one into the blacksmith shop next to the house. The old pickup looked silly, its front end dangling from an A-frame of pine timbers out in the meadow; and when Vera Mae passed it—she had ridden the salt up to the cattle—put her hand on the hard top, it almost raised blisters on her fingertips. She watched June climb off Ruby, and then she took the two sorrels down to the horse pasture bareback and turned them out. All the time Lonnie'd been at the fire she'd looked forward to having a ride with him, she'd put off salting the cattle to have an excuse. Well, June was good company.

She went into the kitchen and made sandwiches of cold biscuits and margarine and peanut butter. She filled a pitcher with powdered lemonade and another one with canned cow and water and chocolate. She opened a can of string beans and made a salad with chopped onions and beans and vinegar and oil. Then she went down to the shop.

Mike greeted her by screeching, "Don't look at the flame, Vera Mae!" He and Lonnie were both wearing goggles.

She said, "I won't. Lunch is ready, Mr. Chevrolet and Mr. Buick."

"I'm Henry Ford," Mike said.

Lonnie turned off the flame and shoved the goggles up on his forehead; sweat ran out of the sponges and streaked his face. "Henry Ford's dead," he said. "Let's eat." He rubbed the small of his back. "My dad built that forge," he said. "Wish he'd set it higher, it and the anvil. He was a short kind of man."

"I'm going to be as big as you," Mike said, shoving his own goggles up.

"I'm going to be exactly Vera Mae's size," June said from the door. "So we can wear each other's clothes."

But Lonnie didn't laugh. He hung his goggles on their hook, racked the nozzle, stared at the welded gear—which still needed cutting and filing—and led the way to the kitchen. His hands greasy with graphite and oil, he poured himself a glass of lemonade, and slouched back from the table. "I ate too much breakfast."

Vera Mae said, "You were hungry a minute ago."

"It just went away." He reached for the saltshaker and poured a couple of spoonfuls on the back of his hand, licked it off; his tongue left a white path in the dirt. "You kids wash up," he said, and stared at his hands. He gulped the lemonade. "I'm goin' to get at it," he said. "Only a couple of hours more. Give me time to get the swill and take it up to the hog pen before supper. If we eat early, I'll have some light to run Bob through the corn and vegetables before full dark. Wanta work on the bathroom tomorrow."

Vera Mae stared at him. It scared her to see Lonnie so tired he couldn't eat. But she knew that she couldn't say anything; she'd never really seen him mad, but he was a man, and he could blow up. So she said, "You've got all day tomorrow, Lonnie."

He wiped his hand across his mouth. The only clean place on him was where the goggles had been. "Promised Old Man Trellis I'd bale alfalfa for him tomorrow afternoon."

"Farming," she said. "For that old skinflint, that pennypincher. What's he paying you, ten cents an hour?"

Lonnie poured another glass of lemonade, and stood up. "When you kids are through eating, ride down to the station, and ask Andy to let me borrow a package of hacksaw blades and a couple of double-o files . . . I ain't hungry." He carried his lemonade out of the kitchen. His feet, in

108

old canvas sneakers, made no noise. But Vera Mae heard the bedsprings creak.

She gave the children an orange and two doughnuts each, and told them they could eat them on the way down to the station. If they were worried about their father, you couldn't tell it from the racket they made as they went out to catch up the sorrels . . . She'd been teaching the two new mares roping, she'd wanted to show Lonnie how good they were getting. Well, next week. She opened a can of soup and heated it, the kerosene stove at once bringing out the sweat all over her body. She carried the soup into the bedroom, pushed a chair over by the bed with her knee and put the soup on it.

Lonnie was lying on the bed, staring at the ceiling with his eyes wide. She sat down beside him and, without saying a word, put her arm under his shoulders and made him sit up. She fed him the first couple of spoonfuls like a kid, and then he took the cup from her and drank the soup down in two gulps. He had always been able to drink things hotter than anybody else; now sweat broke out on his face, and she felt the icy knot in her stomach dissolve.

"You scared me," she said. "You were so hot you couldn't sweat. I thought you had sunstroke."

He shook his head. "I'm just an old boot," he said. "Can't hurt me . . . I feel better, thanks for the soup."

"If you feel better, then you must have felt bad."

"It ain't freezing out in that shop," he said. "And there wasn't any ice under the car . . . Those were a couple of bad fires. I was a sector boss."

"What do they do?" She found a handkerchief in her pocket, and went to the bureau and soaked it in toilet water. Duke and his wife had given her that bottle for her last birthday, and it made her think of her room in their house in the San Fernando Valley. It was a nice room, done in blue and white, and the ceiling was insulated against the heat, there was a panel heater set in the wall for cold days . . .

Lonnie was staring at the ceiling again, but his eyes didn't look so glazed. She cleaned his face with the cologne. "Sector boss?" he asked, coming back from some place. "I supervised three crews. Just walked up and down, telling the crew bosses what to cut and where, maybe taking a lick now and then to show the men how to do it. We had pickup labor, just fellas they hired in the city, not used to the mountains."

"It doesn't sound too bad," Vera Mae said.

"I useta do it on my ear. Maybe I'm getting old."

She laughed. "Maybe you ought to see a doctor, Lonnie."

"Doctor? Me? You taken leave of your senses?"

"One of us has," Vera Mae said. "When a man your age talks about getting old."

"Too old to go to fires," Lonnie said. "I've been fighting fire longer than any brush monkey around here. It useta kind of pep me up, like going to a dance."

"Why, you're a year or so younger than Tommy Burns."

Lonnie looked at her. Then he looked back at the ceiling. "I gotta get out of here and get at that car," he said. "Or Salal Flats'll be getting a new garbage man." But he made no move to sit up. All of a sudden his greasy hand shot out and caught hers and held on so tight that it scared her. "I always said I was a dumb kind of guy. Maybe I'm getting smarter." He shook his head. "I get the rough jobs on fires. The steep sectors, the hot ones. Tommy, he's camp boss, or fire boss, or chief of staff . . . The brass don't kill themelves, and why should they? They can hire us brush monkeys." The hand tightened. "Vera Mae. What you cryin' for?"

"I'm not crying!" she said fiercely. She pushed at her face with the grease-streaked, cologne-smelling handkerchief. "I'm not! Oh, Lonnie, I did that to you! Tommy was your good friend, and I acted stinking to him and his goddamned wife and—"

At once he sat up and swung his feet to the floor; his

arm went around her. "You're crazy! I wasn't talking about that at all. I was all of a sudden gettin' smart! It's always been that way, the brass gotta look out for themselves. They're gonna be fighting fire the rest of their lives, till they retire. If they took it rough, like we do, they wouldn't last."

They sat on the edge of the bed, their arms around each other. "You've got to quit, Lonnie. Resign or retire or whatever it is—"

He shook his head. "I can't. Look, baby. Pack up, get outa here. I—I never had the right to bring you into this. I—ain't it funny? Just last year, I useta work all night, and all day too and come back after— Once I went on a fire that lasted twenty-one days. During the war, when they was really short of trained men. Don't remember sleeping at all, but I guess I did . . . Came home and slept seven hours—it was raining, that's what put the fire out—and got up the next morning to work on the pipe line, carried—I thought, sure, some day you'll get old, worn down, but it was—I dunno—ten, twenty years away."

He stood up, rubbing his hands. "I better start cutting those gears. C'mon out with me."

She followed him out to the blacksmith shop. She had never been so scared in her life. Lonnie still stood straight and muscular and—well, wonderful-looking—but his face called his body a liar; he looked whipped. She watched him build a little fire in the forge, and she stepped over and automatically started turning the bellows handle for him.

He put the newly welded gear in and began to turn it with his tongs. When it was white hot, he laid it on the anvil and began hammering it, his back supple and straight, the muscles in his forearm flowing smooth as water. He finished, and laid the part on the anvil. "Let it cool slow," he said. "When the kids come back I'll cut the teeth and file them, and the car'll be better than new."

She said, "How do you know how deep to cut them?"

"I'm smart," Lonnie said. He rubbed his forearm over

111

his brow. "I kept an old gear that cracked. I'll use it for a pattern." He laughed. "Had so damn many V-8's, got almost every kind of part on hand with something a little wrong with it. Just try and find two with different things wrong, an' weld 'em together . . . Here come the kids." He looked out. "Somebody who's been on a horse before's been training those mares. Indians, I guess, sneakin' in here at night."

This was the Lonnie she knew. As he tightened the vise down on the gears and took a file from Mike, he began whistling "No Letter Today."

At two o'clock, Vera Mae and June and Mike stood by like the owners of the Cunard line watching the launching of the *Queen Mary*. Lonnie got behind the wheel of the pickup and released the emergency; he switched on the juice, threw her in high, and coasted forward. The motor caught, and he threw in the clutch and held her on the footbrake while he gunned the motor hot with the hand throttle; then slowly, and with his lips clenched tight, he put her into low. Even more slowly he drew back on the clutch pedal; without undue noise the car went into low gear; and all of a sudden, Lonnie gave her the gas and started driving around the meadow in low, cutting figure eights like he was working a cowpony, and laughing like a loon. Mike jumped in next to his father, and June started yelling, "Vera Mae'n I'll ride Bob down! We'll meet you at Mark's place!" and the Verdoux ranch was itself again. Almost.

D RIVING DOWN to the ranger station, Vera Mae realized that low gear had been making an awful lot of noise an awful long time; now that it had stopped, it was surprising she hadn't noticed it before. But even if she had, what could she have done about it? Not made a new gear herself; and certainly not taken the pickup to a garage, and the prices they charge.

Be funny to do that. Probably wasn't a garage around used to working on cars so old, so honestly wore out. Probably didn't even stock parts for 36's.

She parked where the signs said for the public to park. Lonnie always drove on in over the cattle guard, acting like their old hack was a government car, but she wasn't Lonnie.

She told the kids to go play; there was a lot for them to do, everyone on the station was a friend of theirs. But she wasn't Mike or June, either.

She turned right, went away from the office, and toward the big house with the porch furniture and the curtains in the window.

The walks on the station were fieldstone, joined together with wide strips of mortar; they made bad walking for her high heels, she could feel the rough surface on the stones through her thin-soled pumps.

She went up on the porch, and wished there was some place to hide; she wanted to look in a mirror, her nose must be shiny, her mascara had surely run, her hair was probably every way but right. But there wasn't any place to go, and she could be seen from the windows; so she just knocked on the door.

Almost at once Dot's voice called out, "Come in," but

113

she waited, and then she heard moccasins or slippers—she couldn't be sure—shuffling across the floor, and Dot's thin figure appeared darkly among the shadows on the other side of the screen door.

Dot's voice said, "Oh. It's you," and then Vera Mae was inside, unable to see anything, giddy in the gloom after the blinding sun on the lawns and walks outside. "You've got a dress on," Dot said.

Vera Mae said, "It's a social call. All of a sudden I was caught up on my housework, so I put a dress on and decided to make a social call."

Her eyes were focusing now, and she could see that Dot's face was shiny with sweat, her hair was stringy. Vera Mae said, "I stole some money from the housekeeping. Why don't you get dressed up, and we'll go downtown? I haven't been in town since I don't know when."

The ranger's wife said, "I was ironing the bedroom curtains," but she sounded uncertain. "I like your dress."

"Let's see what you have, so we can dress to match." Suddenly Vera Mae giggled and as suddenly the other girl joined in.

"I can't see in this light, is that black or midnight?"

Vera Mae said, "Navy . . . If you had something red?"

"But I have. Red butcher linen. My mother sent it to me for my birthday." The giggle was real now. "You go phone Mark to see Mike and June have lunch while I take a bath." She was already pulling her T-shirt over her head as she went into the bedroom. She wasn't wearing a bra.

By the time Vera Mae had figured out the switchboard that stood at the kitchen door, Dot was back, pulling the red linen over her head. "I even put stockings on." She stood up to have her back buttoned, running a careless comb through her hair.

"Let's swap belts," Vera Mae said. "When I was in high school my girl friend and I always did that when we double-dated." She took off her wide white leather belt and put it around Dot's waist. "No soap," she said. "My

114

golly, and I thought I had a small waist. Yours must be twenty-four."

"And a half," Dot said. "Difference is, you curve a little other places."

"A little too much," Vera Mae said.

"Not at all," Dot said. "You have a lovely figure." And all at once they were being polite again, and it was all going to fall apart before Vera Mae could do anything toward what she'd swallowed her pride to do.

She said, "Mark was full of curiosity. But I didn't tell him a thing."

"Oh, sure," Dot said carelessly. "Being a ranger's wife is like living in a goldfish bowl." But she said it nicely. "Well, I robbed my housekeeping money, too. Let's go. We'll take my car."

"I'll have to move ours then," Vera Mae said. "The battery'll be dead when we get back, and I didn't park on a hill."

"I'll give you a push to start you," Dot said. "The bumpers are just the same."

Her car was a '38 Ford coupe, but it was in a lot better shape than the Verdoux truck. It had lived an honest life, doing only what its maker had meant it to do, just carrying a couple and sometimes their friends around; it had never hauled garbage, lumber, sand, cement or hay, except in small, family-size loads.

It had a good battery, too; turned the motor right over, and made it say uncle. They rattled out across the cattle ground.

"I feel like a jerk," Vera Mae said, "not taking the kids."

Dot said, "Yeah. Well, they'll have a good time. Andy's got the crew drilling, they can help."

"They're such good kids, it seems a shame not to do everything I can for them. I don't deserve them."

"No," Dot said flatly. She took the car around a lumber truck expertly, and now they were on the last grade down to town.

This, Vera Mae thought, is earning anything I get the hard way. This is worse than anything I ever did for a drink and a dinner when I was following the rodeo. This is the prime, first-grade, select queen of the jerks.

She said, "June's birthday is pretty soon. I'll have to come to you for advice about a present."

"All the girls do," Dot said. "They say I have very good taste. I don't know, I think it's just being willing to think about things. And I do read all the women's magazines for hints. Do you read much?"

Vera Mae said she was afraid she didn't. "Mark Somers is a great reader, isn't he?"

"Oh," Dot said. "That dry old stuff. He reads all the government pamphlets, everything. It's just a nervous habit."

And that, thought Vera Mae, is that. They were in town now, the car slowing down for traffic, the big wide street busy with trucks and cars and even two horse-drawn wagons. Dot was clever cutting into the curb and parking diagonally. "Maury's is the best place to eat in town. Do you want to windowshop first or afterwards?"

"Let's eat," Vera Mae said. "I want to see if other people's cooking is as much better than mine as I remember it."

"I've got a good cookbook I'll loan you," Dot said.

The restaurant was air-conditioned, and plants grew on the top of the partition between the beer bar and the eating tables. Dot sat down facing the door, and Vera Mae slid in opposite her. "Too bad you can't get a cocktail with your lunch here," Dot said. "That was the nicest part of eating lunch in San Francisco."

"I've never been much of a hand to drink in daylight," Vera Mae said. Then she was sorry she'd said it; she didn't dare criticize Dot.

But you couldn't, not and have the ranger's wife know it.

116

"Alcohol's never been a problem in my family," Dot said.

Vera Mae managed not to giggle, thinking of her book-keeper father, her choirlady mother.

The waitress showed up. "We'll have fried shrimps," Dot said, "and the chef's salad." The waitress went away again, her orders received.

With the shrimps, Dot got positively genial. "Tommy says Lon is doing wonderful work with his spike camp. Only he'd kill me if he knew I'd told you."

She smiled, and something in her smile told Vera Mae that the thin girl was, amazingly, trying to be nice. "Lon's different," Dot said. "You can tell him he's good, and he doesn't right away expect a brass badge and a permanent appointment. I guess you were right about him, he really is serious about the ranch, isn't he?"

Vera Mae reminded herself that Dot had gone an awfully long way to make friends. She drank ice water—the first in months—and said, "He's a hard worker."

Dot said, "Men are such boys, aren't they? It's up to us to take them seriously and make them feel good."

Vera Mae kept her voice level as she said, "I wish some of the old gals from the rodeo were here. They'd never believe this."

Dot didn't get anything she wasn't supposed to get. She said, "This must be a terrible change for you."

"Yeah," Vera Mae said. She devoted herself to her food. It tasted fine, no matter who was sitting across from her. She didn't even mind when Dot made her take back a dime of the money she had meant to leave for a tip. She put the coin back down when Dot's back was turned.

Outside, the street was baking in the early afternoon sun. Sweat ran down Vera Mae's sides; no doubt Dot perspired. They looked in the window of a jewelry store, and Dot said she thought it was vulgar to wear Indian silver; they looked in a dress shop, and Dot said that necklines were going to be lower than ever this year; they looked in

117

a lingerie window, and neither of them was interested. Then Dot looked at some junk which she called bree-a-braw, which Vera Mae guessed was right, without caring much; and then they had a soda, because neither of them had to worry about her figure.

At three o'clock there wasn't anything left to do in town. They bought some canned goods and bacon, because town prices were cheaper than Salal Flats, and put their two paper cartons in the turtle back, and the car started up as good this time as it had before.

The road was beginning to climb off the flat on which the town was built before Vera Mae thought it was tactful to bring up the subject she was interested in. "Lonnie's sure getting to a lot of fires this summer."

"Yes," Dot said. "Tommy gives him every chance he can. It really isn't fair to Tommy, having his best guard gone so much, but he's awfully loyal to his guards; he wants them to make as much money as possible, even if it does leave him shorthanded."

"It leaves me shorthanded, too," Vera Mae said. "He doesn't get home enough to help me much."

"I'll tell you what," Dot said. Her face was bright against the scrub oak background; she was conferring a favor. "There's a little apartment off the barracks, two bedrooms and a bath; I'll get Tommy to let you use it. It'll make things much easier for you."

Vera Mae was so surprised she forgot to be tactful. "And let the ranch go?"

"Oh, pooh," Dot said. "That's what us gals know. You could be tactful and all, and pretty soon Lonnie'd think it was his idea to abandon that old patch of sagebrush. I'll bet he wishes he could, without having to back down from all his brags about making a ranch."

Vera Mae couldn't say anything. She watched the car climb from the foothills; live oak to black oak, firs to ponderosa pines, and the cedars in between. Wasn't a tree she didn't know, and most of the bushes, too.

118

Dot was happy with her philanthropy. "As long as Tommy and I are here, you could use the apartment even winters, when Lon's not working for the service . . . And you wouldn't have to give up the ranch altogether. Old Man Trellis would pay the taxes if he could have the graze, he's always ready to do that . . . We could fix over your cabin, it would be dandy for overnight picnics."

Vera Mae kept her temper down. "I don't think Lonnie would want to let the ranch go bare."

Dot was silent awhile. "I know. Joan used to try and get him to. But sometimes I thought he and Joan didn't get along so well, and you, I mean, a new wife . . . Though I've only been married once, I've no authority to talk . . . Lonnie's about the most independent guard I know. It's just too bad he couldn't have had an education, he'd have made a fine ranger, Tommy says . . . Maybe if he studied, he could be a dispatcher, lots of them work the year round."

"Maybe," Vera Mae said.

"Because, of course, these little ranches around here aren't worth a thing. Not on any ranger district I ever saw. I'll give you a pamphlet; probably Lonnie already has a copy from Tommy or Mark, that's how the National Forests came about, they are to take care of the land that isn't worth anything except as public watersheds or—or something. Tommy'd have to tell you."

They passed the Salal Flats store, thank God, and pretty soon she would be out of this car. There wasn't anything she could say, without making it worse. And the hell of it was, she knew that Dot meant well. Dot really believed all that stuff she was still putting out, about how there weren't enough people living in all the mountains of the West to make Congress interested, and without a subsidy how could you live on something that was marked submarginal land in 1903?

"Of course Lonnie's a dear, and he's tried so hard," Dot said. "With that horse and all, the one that turned out to

119

be a killer. If it had been anybody but Lonnie, the sheriff would have investigated, because whoever heard of anyone getting rich off a wild horse, but that's Lon for you. He's really tough. Tommy says, the last man to hold on to a homestead here, and the oldest fire-fighting guard on the forest; it gets most of them long before this, you know."

Vera Mae said feebly, "Tommy's almost as old as Lon, Dot."

Dot slowed down for the ranger station. "But he's brass, dear. And while working with your head is really harder at fires, all the responsibility and all, they do come back faster, I know."

She stopped in the public parking lot, edged her front bumper to the back bumper of the old pickup. Vera Mae got out and got her box of groceries and put it in the back seat. "Thanks a lot, Dot. I had a time."

"Didn't we just, dear? And it was your idea. How about the children?"

"I hear them down behind the station," Vera Mae said. She had the worst headache of her life. "Even if I have to stop, there are hills back there."

"We must do this again," Dot said. Vera Mae climbed into the pickup, Dot gunned her motor, and the good old loyal Verdoux car started on the first bump.

She drove across the cattle guard after Dot, and began honking her horn for the kids. She wanted to get back to the ranch.

She wanted to get back and start working. At anything that showed up. She was going to forget everything that had happened today. She was going to forget that she'd even thought of asking Lonnie's boss to give him an easier job, and she was going to try and forget—if she could—that Lonnie had a boss.

VERA MAE worked the horses. There was some profit in buying green broke mares like the sorrels and turning them into cowponies; some profit, but not a very sure one, because a sale depended on having the ponies where and when somebody wanted to buy a stock horse. In the back country nobody but Old Man Trellis ran cattle any more, and he raised his own horses; so you would have to wait for a rodeo or a passing dude, or you would have to have a trailer if you didn't want to just ship your finished horses to a dealer and take a chance that his feed bill wouldn't eat up your sale price.

Still and all, it was a poor kind of hand who'd leave a horse second-rate when he had the time to improve him; so Vera Mae worked the sorrels every afternoon. Once when the kids had gone to a PTA picnic she got out her old trick-saddle with the hand holds, and tried to train Ruby to let Vera Mae go under her belly, but she couldn't do it; she kept seeing the faces of June and Mike—and Lonnie—if they found her in the meadow with her neck broken.

The pigs grew like pigs, and the cattle slowly worked their way through one gate after another to the high country at the head of the canyon; they put on their quiet pounds, and nothing real bad happened to any of them, nothing that Vera Mae or Lonnie—or once Stan Trellis on horse patrol, riding Betsy—couldn't fix with a quick rope and a bottle of bone remedy.

Lonnie went to a few fires—the worst one lasted three days and two nights—and he ran up a little overtime, which was all to the good. On the way home from the three-day fire somebody bought a bottle, but Lon offered to drive the car instead of taking a drink; he wasn't off the stuff, but he'd decided it didn't mix with fire fighting. "You boys come around after the first rain, and I'll drink you broke."

He didn't ever get around to finishing the bathroom because the second lieu day of each pair he spent working for Old Man Trellis—baling hay, cutting silage, mending fence, pouring a cement floor in the slaughterhouse. If he got paid for this, Vera Mae never saw the money, but she knew better than to ask—if Lonnie owed Old Man Trellis for something, if he was making money toward a surprise for her, that was his business. If a man's got it to do, he's got it to do.

Things were as good as they could be, with Lonnie away from home five nights a week and sometimes more. Even that didn't bother her so much, because the vegetables started getting ripe—string beans and then tomatoes, first a few every day and then in a red flood. She put them up in glass jars, cases of them at a time, working in the ranch kitchen without a hot water faucet, working at night till the lamps and the stove combined to make the kitchen so hot the tomatoes almost cooked in their lug boxes. When she got through, she was glad Lonnie was away; she wouldn't want any man to see her or her kitchen the way she left them when she went to bed.

Potatoes were coming ripe, too. They didn't have a horse-drawn potato digger, so Mark was taking care of them; he dug her potatoes, she canned his beans and vegetables. Lonnie had a root cellar where they kept the potatoes and turnips; he said there was a way of keeping cabbage there, too, only cabbage wouldn't be ready for a while, and maybe they'd make sauerkraut out of it anyway.

Pheasant season came in, and Lonnie got her a license and she carried an old 16-gauge shotgun in a saddle boot. She tried to teach the mares to let her shoot from the saddle; but she never did get any place with it; Lonnie had trained Bob, and she used him, or, if she was on Ruby or

Sweetie, she got down to shoot. She was pretty good, and she and the kids ate pheasant and tomatoes, beans and potatoes until they ran out of their ears.

Lonnie showed up in Mark's pickup one night; it was maybe a month after the terrible day when he had complained of being too tired to eat, when he had worried about growing old and weak. "They want some fellows on a fire clear down at the south end of the region," he said. "Tommy said me and Mark could go if we wanted to make the extra money. Mark here says he won't go without me. We don't have to. It's just that they want three men from this forest altogether. Red Rock's sending one, and they'll send more."

It was toward sunset; the red light was strong on the brown meadow grass, and Vera Mae, leaning an elbow on the pickup door, squinted. "Why ask me? They don't need a tomato canner, do they?"

Mark said, "This time of year, you get one of those west-side, southern forests they may not release you for a long time."

Lonnie said, "Gov'ment puts out money for a trip on a real plane, they figure to get it back. This isn't one of those cheap C-47 deals."

"Tommy won't usually lend me out," Mark said. "But they need a timekeeper bad . . . She's run three thousand acres already, she's going to be a big one."

Vera Mae began to laugh. "You look like June and Mike when they want to play instead of stringing beans. I'm not your mama, boys. G'wan and go."

Mark said, "It leaves you stuck with the patch, just when everything's coming on. It isn't right. But let's say yes before she changes her mind, Lonnie."

He reached out and switched the radio on. He raised headquarters in the city and told them he and Verdoux would be down at the airport by eleven o'clock. He switched off, and said, "Pretty elegant. I never traveled on an airliner before." He got out of the car. "No hurry.

Think I'll ask the kids what they want for a present." He walked down toward the beaver dam; it didn't need a map to find out where Mike and June were whooping at each other.

As soon as he was out of earshot, she said at once, "If this is a particularly dangerous job you're going on, don't tell me about it."

Lonnie laughed. He looked at Mark Somers' retreating back and then grabbed her up. "Naw. Less'n most of 'em. It's just that I don't have to go this time. I got a free choice." He grinned down at her. "In this family, that means, we got a choice."

She said, "You want to go. That's good enough for me. Always will be. I wouldn't give you a plugged nickel for a man who had to run to his wife to see if he could blow his nose."

Lonnie said, "I wouldn't either—a couple of months ago. Never figured I'd have the kind of wife I got . . . Listen, baby. I got it to tell you. There isn't a damn thing I wouldn't do for you, up to and including pushing a cholla cactus uphill with my nose."

She leaned back in his arms and looked up at him. "Now you are scaring me. You and Mark plan on running off with a couple of airline hostesses?"

"I hear," Lonnie looked thoughtful, "that they're all good-lookin', and they're cheap feeds for fear of gaining weight. Also, they make big money."

She laughed. "I'm not scared now. You're all right. But why the big good-by?"

He looked over her head. His hands dropped from around her. There was very little lift in his voice as he said, "It's no good saying things about people who are dead. Joan was always after me to make more money, and then sore 'cause I had to go away to do it." He shook his head. "I felt bad all the time, because I felt I ought to move into town, where I could work and stay home. I

124

kept wondering what kind of man I was, to put a piece of land above my wife."

"What is this leading up to, Lonnie? You're my kind of man, is all I know."

He said, "That's good enough for me . . . What I'm trying to say is, tomorrow, on my lieu day, was supposed to be special. Now I'm flyin' off instead."

"Lonnie, we're doing so good. All that food put away, the mares shaping up good, the pigs and cows all fine, and you getting the government to owe you big money. I wouldn't swap with Mr. King of the King Ranch."

He laughed. "Well, I hate missin' your face when you get your surprise. You been wondering what I was doing, giving up half my lieu time to Old Man Trellis, and never getting a cent from him?"

She said, "The way Old Man Trellis is, God almighty couldn't get more than a cent."

He got his arms around her again. There was hardly any twilight left, and Mark and the kids were coming back. "I'm a dumb kind of son, but I figgered out there was one thing you wanted. By your brag to Duke and all. So—I swapped Old Man my time for a while against that Steeldust stud he calls Prince. You want to be in the horse-raising business, I'm the man'll put you in. He's all yours, sealed, signed and delivered; just ride on down and pick him up. Stan'll be by for you on his patrol."

She said, "Oh, Lonnie," because it would break his heart if she was ungrateful. She stood on tiptoes and kissed him as hard as she could. She told herself that if he ever found out that she hated this Prince before she ever saw him, she hoped her tongue'd be cut out and thrown to the hogs.

She called herself a romantic little fool, and some worse names. My God, what difference did it make? She had Lonnie, and June and Mike, she had a beautiful ranch, the money from the Forest Service was as good as in the bank. And she was sad because as long as this—this second-

125

hand horse Prince was in the stallion corral, there was no room on the ranch for even a dream of the horse they called Mulemouth—the most beautiful, most—well, just most—wild stallion in the world.

The horse that Lonnie had caught for his first wife, and never apparently had even thought of catching for her.

CHAPTER X

PRINCE WAS eighteen years old, red roan, and what they call Steeldust in the hills, a loose term that means just about what quarter horse does in more sophisticated circles. The original Steeldust was a Morgan stallion that the Army sent out to improve the breed of Southwestern broncos; but from the number of towns who now claim that the original Steeldust used to stand there, he must have been a horse named Legion. Nowadays, in the back country, any breedy-looking stock horse whose ancestry is unknown is called a Steeldust.

He was sixteen-one, chunky-built, and real proud in the head. A lot of people around there could remember when he was one hell of a roping and cutting horse; he would have won all the blue ribbons and medals and cups in the state if Old Man Trellis had believed in such fofarrow as rodeos and horse shows and county fairs.

But about eight years ago Prince had been hurt when a trailer-hitch broke, and he was stiff in the hind legs. This didn't hurt him as a saddle horse; and it had nothing at all to do with his powers as a stallion, which Old Man Trellis pointed out. "This yere is a goronteed stud. If he don't get any colts fer you, Mrs. Verdoux, Lonnie gets his money back. He won't rope any more, mind you, and I wouldn't turn him on no dimes in no muddy country; but fer what you want him, he'll throw you as nice colts as there is within ten miles of here." Prince was the only stallion for ten miles around. "Wouldn't be gettin' rid of him if he wasn't daddy to three-fourths of the mares on this ranch."

"Also granddaddy and great-granddaddy," Stan said. He smoothed his nice green tie. "The Old Man believes in sticking to a good thing when you get it. Want me to saddle for you, Vera Mae?"

Vera Mae said, "Just throw my saddle on the ground, and I'll hang around getting acquainted with Prince before I ride him home."

"Gentle as a kitten," Old Man Trellis said. "If you just remember he's a stud and therefore notional . . . And goronteed. Of course, seein' that this wasn't a cash deal, Lonnie couldn't expect cash back if Prince doesn't live up to specifications. But Stan'll work a day back for every day Lonnie worked."

"No matter who does what around this place," Stan said, "I get it in the neck . . . But I think this is a safe deal, Vera Mae. Prince caught three out of four of our mares this season. Otherwise, I'd put my foot down, and not out of consideration for you and Lon. I got no great urge to spend my lieu days helping Lonnie put in that bathroom."

"Lieu days," Old Man Trellis snorted. He put a hand on Prince's corral rail and leaned against it, comfortably. "Ain't gonna be many more lieu days; gonna be an early fall. I kin smell rain two weeks off, and I bin smelling it a piece now . . . All you able-bodied men layin' around on the gov'ment's time gonna have to go to work. Well, mebbe-so it'll cut the income tax next year." The rail he leaned on was fresh cut pine; the Old Man inspected a blob of pitch on his hand, and used it to stick down a tear in his leather jacket.

Vera Mae walked up to the stud and put out her hand. He snuffled at it like an old Shetland pony and was quiet while she ran her hand under his chin and then back and over his neck and head. She said, "I can handle him," and reached for her saddle.

Stan got out of his pickup and saddled for her; he slid the stallion's bridle on. His father said, "Lonnie didn't say nothing about the bridle—"

Vera Mae said, "Next time you have a flat tire I'll change it for you." The Old Man's son laughed; the Old Man grunted. Vera Mae stepped into the saddle and turned toward the road. Stan passed her a ways down the road, and when she got to the entrance to the Trellis place, he was waiting with the gate open.

She rode through and then wheeled the stud around; she forgot, and turned too sharply, and the Prince almost fell. She picked him up with the reins and said, "You can't see the gate from the house, can you, Stan?"

He latched the gate and stood by the green car, looking up at her. "Yeah?"

"Your wife and your mother wouldn't like if it they saw you meeting me here."

He said, "For God's sake, Vera Mae. Get the chip off your shoulder."

"They never came out of the house all the time I was talking to you two."

"Well, no," Stan Trellis said. "Since you asked for it. They think you think you're too good for them. Because you went to one PTA meeting and haven't been seen since, except sucking up to the ranger's wife. I don't mind telling you, it makes me a little sick. Lonnie's always been a friend of mine, I looked forward to you and us going around together some. There are damn few people to talk to back here."

Vera Mae sat easy in the saddle. Prince snorted a little to remind her he was a stallion, and then stood loose, shifting his weight to rest each of his back legs in turn. "What do you hang around here for?"

Stan Trellis said: "Because some day the Old Man'll give up and let me run this place. Hell, he's a mean old

128

coot, and a skinflinting penny-pincher, but he's my family . . . There's Tommy, there's Clint Clinto and Mark Somers, and some others for friends. I like this country, I plan to live here quite a long time. It made me feel good to see somebody move up here that'd be fun to talk to. Then you gotta snoot everybody within fifty miles."

"My, my," Vera Mae said. "What a long speech."

"Oh, go to hell," Stan Trellis said. He got in the pickup and drove off. Vera Mae started up the highway on her stiff-legged, high-built stud. She remembered to keep to the shoulder; where there wasn't any, at the waterbreaks, she raised the reins high for control. Prince was in no condition to stop himself if his unshod hoofs started sliding on the pavement.

Once or twice cars passed her—a beer truck, an out-of-state sedan—and she was uncomfortable, being seen on such a lousy horse. Then, at once, she was ashamed. She remembered Lonnie dragging himself down to serve his time with Old Man Trellis for this present; remembered the awful day when his strength had faltered. Half his time for all of fire season, and she was ashamed of what it had bought her!

Riding up the highway, out in sight of the world—if the world had been driving over the back country that day—Vera Mae started to cry. The tears ran down her face, and she let them run, while Prince stiff-leggedly walked toward his new home.

When she went by the ranger station, where Andy Anderson held down the office while Mark was away, she could hear the kids down at the playground between the nine-car garage and the creek. But she didn't turn in. She remembered the day Duke had brought the new mares up, and the way Mike and June had carried on.

But she didn't think that they'd be any too favorable to showing their new horse off to the rest of the kids at the PTA picnic. Or maybe their new mama, either, who was

129

the only woman in the back country that hadn't turned anything in to the lunch that all the children were about to eat . . .

So she just rode on by.

CHAPTER XI

WHEN THE KIDS got up, they ran outside first thing; then they ran back in again, in their pyjamas, shouting, "He's coming home, he's coming home!"

Vera Mae in her nightgown rushed out. But they weren't pointing down the road but to the southwest. The sky there was black for the first time since she'd come to the back country; but up here the sun was up, warm and gentle—in fact, warmer than the morning had been for a long time. A gentle, soothing wind blew in from the southwest; when you looked, you saw that all kinds of things were moving around that ordinarily sat still even in high winds, because they had piled up, sheltered from the devil winds and the prevailing due-west wind, but not from the southwest rain wind.

Mike yipped, "Pop'll be home now," he said. "There comes the rain!"

June, more sedate, said, "Maybe his plane won't be able to land in the rain."

"Plane?" Mike laughed. "Forest Service'll send him up in a bus, now he's not going to a fire." They ran around the house toward the back, their bare feet drumming on the summer-packed dirt. For the twelve days Lonnie'd been gone, they had been a passenger airliner and a C-47, interchangeably; now they would probably be Greyhound buses all day.

She went back into the bedroom, stripped off her night-

130

gown, got into blue jeans and a cotton shirt. Warm today. It was hard to think that rain was coming, she had never seen it. But Lonnie had talked about it, and Mark, and even Mike; the first fall rain. Ten days ago Old Man Trellis had said it.

She fried bacon and beat up pancake batter; mixed the milk, set the table. Let's see. Cover the hay stacked down by the breaking corral. How about Prince? If she let him out, he went for Bob, chasing the cowhorse away from the mares, until both of them were run thin. If she left him in the breaking corral without cover, he'd get wet. The other horses could run loose in the horse pasture, they had trees to get under. But the poor stiff old bast—

She'd have to bring him up to the barn. Which meant she'd have to move his hay. Well, maybe a bale would do, and Lonnie'd be home to help move the rest. But if the rain kept up, they couldn't drive around, the pickup'd stick in the mud and—

She called out, "Mike, how long does the first fall rain last?"

Mike never unbuttoned all the buttons of his shirt at night, and in the morning he slipped it over his head. Now his voice came from the kids' room, muffled. "One day, maybe two . . . I ain't sure, Vera Mae. I was pretty little last year."

She'd move one bale. She'd open it up and throw the pillows into the car one at a time, put them in one stall and Prince in another. But first she'd get breakfast . . .

By ten o'clock she had Prince and a week's feed moved up to the barn. Shut in the small stall he squealed his discontent; but he didn't kick; perhaps he couldn't. She gave Bob and the sorrels an extra feed of grain, and some hay; they might have trouble grazing in the rain. She hauled two gunnysacks of corn to the hogs for the same reason. She put the kids to dragging out of the barn every piece of tarpaulin they could find and stretching it in the sun.

131

At quarter of twelve she stopped to smoke a cigarette and take a breath. The sun was still warm, gently so; the rocks felt hot to the touch, but her skin was not dry and harsh . . .

The light was peculiar; it had a looking-glass quality. When you stared at the trees in the meadow, it was almost like you could see part of the back of the trunk.

The black front of the rain clouds was only half as far away as it had been that morning.

The children were tired out from working; they ate their lunch quietly, and argued with each other about who had done most, but they argued in sleepy, dulled voices. She told them they had to take naps after lunch, and they hardly protested. They were asleep before they took their clothes off.

The black front was steadily coming toward her. There was nothing threatening about it; rain was needed, wanted, and friendly. But they had to be ready for it.

She used Bob and a rope to haul a tarp down to the breaking corral and cover the hay she'd bought and left there. When she went by the barn Prince squealed and tried to come over the top of the Dutch door after the gelding; Bob curvetted under the saddle, and she had trouble keeping her rope clear. But spurs drove the horse on, and she got the hay covered.

She used him again to take a cover to the little wood-cutting outfit Lonnie had standing up on the other side of the creek. When she crossed above the beaver pond, she could hear tails slapping; the beavers must have known high water was coming, and were strengthening their dams against it.

The tarps to cover the corncrib had to be moved only fifty feet, and she tried it by hand. But her fingernails broke and her hands got sore at once; she went back to using the horse, mad at herself because she wasn't bigger and stronger and had to waste all that time climbing in and out of a saddle. The corncrib was high, over her head, and she had to throw her line over a tree limb and use Bob's strength to raise the canvas.

Even then, it was devilish work spreading the tarps.

At two o'clock Mike appeared in the door of the cabin, and then June. They started laughing. "Look at yourself, Vera Mae. Look in the mirror!"

Because she needed their help and didn't want to waste time, she stepped into the kitchen. In the glass over the sink she saw a witch: mildew-streaked face, hair in long straggles of sweaty rope, one eye unaccountably ringed in green. She could not remember having anything to do with any green dirt.

She said, "Let's see who can get dirtiest," and sent them to get the two sorrels under saddle and up here to help her. There was still Lonnie's precious plumbing outfit to cover. And the milled lumber to build the bathroom. And three sacks of cement. She either had to cover them or get them into the barn, and the sacks were made of paper and couldn't be dragged.

When the sorrels came up, they couldn't be worked. Ruby was in season and kept dancing away toward the barn where Prince now kept up a steady trumpeting and squealing. Whatever had hurt his legs hadn't done his chest and throat any harm. So she wasted time making Mike take them back—June wanted to go with him—and put June on Bob to haul and hold two sacks of potatoes up and under oak limbs while Vera Mae tied them off. This was so rough that she dragged a sack of onions into the kitchen instead of hanging it.

Now it turned out the kids had left their saddles down at the horse gate. Rather than climb down and tie Bob, start the pickup and drive down there—all that getting in and out—she loped to the horse pasture and made a pickup, rodeo style, riding the saddle back to the barn and throwing it over the Dutch door with a flip of Bob's hindquarters.

But that meant two trips, and now the light was fading.

133

There was the blackness of dusk on the ranch, made stronger by the golden sunshine still lying on the sagebrush toward the desert. The breeze, which had been steady and gentle and warm picked up into little gusts that blew one way and then the other; she thought she felt a drop hit her hand. But it might have been sweat from her face, or lather from Bob's bits.

She sat in her saddle, bone-tired, dead. The kids looked up at her, and even Mike was too pooped to grab a stirrup and climb up behind her. In the barn, that damn Prince snorted and banged his stall.

"What now?" she asked. "We all gotta put our heads on it. What's uncovered?"

"The pigs?" June asked.

Vera Mae shook her head. "Pigs like mud. Let 'em stay out."

Mike twisted his toes inward. She knew the look; he had something to say, and was afraid to say it. She leaned from the saddle. "Spit it out, pal. I like bad news."

"Well—" Mike looked at the ground. "Well—I ain't sure—but Pop always opens the water breaks on the road, and moves the cows into the dry field. That is, he usually does, when it starts raining."

Vera Mae nodded. "I mighta knowed," she said. "Couldn't live on a ranch all this time and never get my hands around a shovel." But they didn't laugh; four big eyes in two small faces stared at her mournfully. It occurred to her that they were sorry for her. She said briskly, "Well, you two get a shovel and start down the road to the gate. I'll ride up the pasture, and turn the cows."

Mike said hesitantly, "I could do that. Open the gap up the canyon, an' the cows'll go through, they been wantin' to get at that grass a long time."

This time there was no question where the drop of water had come from; the first spatter of the fall rain. The blackness had almost reached the sagebrush now; the trees were humming with the steady wind, no longer gusty but

134

no longer a breeze, either. Vera Mae stared at the sky. She was losing a lot of time, trying to make up her mind. "You two got slickers?"

They ran yipping for the cabin. She rode—oh, God—for the horse pasture and got Sweetie, mad because she shouldn't have sent her back in the first place. Ruby fought to get out and get to Prince, and she batted the sorrel nose with her hat, and left Ruby raising hell, with her last friend gone.

She saddled Sweetie herself. There was no damn reason to send both children up the canyon, but she wasn't going to break June's heart to keep from saddling a horse.

The brats came tumbling toward her, their tiredness forgotten, laughing like a pair of clowns; they had grown so much in the last year that their slickers didn't fit. She put Mike's on June, and found an old city raincoat of hers for Mike; she wrenched the tail till it split, so it could be worn in the saddle. They went loping toward the gate and the canyon on Bob and Sweetie, and the rain was a real drizzle now, steady and determined.

When they had gone out of sight over the rise, she felt lonely for the first time in weeks. She picked up the long-handled round-point shovel—which Lonnie, Forest Service style, usually gave its full title—and shouldered it. Lonnie had told her never to carry a tool that way, for some reason that escaped her.

The rain felt good; her hat protected her face, her leather jacket protected her shoulders, but an occasional gust would come along and it felt cool; she took her free hand and rubbed the water around on her dirty face. She could get soaked, and what the hell; light the kerosene range and put her clothes to dry, and run around the house in something else. Her man'd be home tonight, there couldn't be a forest fire going in the whole West Coast.

She reached the gate and checked automatically to see if the kids had closed it good; they had. She started back.

Lonnie had pointed out the water breaks to her, with that interest in every clod of dirt on the ranch that had been touching and lovable a couple of months ago. But now that she wanted to find them, they weren't so easy to locate; ditches left across the road to let the water run off and over the surface, keep the ruts from catching the whole runoff. You filled them in the summer to save your springs, and you had to dig them out before anything but a light summer storm, or the fill would act as a dam that backed up and undercut the road, and you could be cut off all winter that way. But the fill would be loose and easily kicked off the road . . .

All you had to do, in the words of the old story, was think where you would go if you were water. She picked a nice low place that seemed like it would drain quite an area and pushed the shovel down. It wouldn't go.

She pushed the arch of her boot against it, and the shovel slipped on the damp clay and skidded and nearly threw her. About three aches developed in her back, and when she tried again, something went wrong with her arrangement of hat and jacket collar, and a cool stream of water went down her neck. She tried to tell herself it was refreshing, but without success.

By scraping and pushing, and sometimes succeeding in digging a real shovelful, she got the first water break open. Or thought she did. Though the drizzle had turned to rain now, there wasn't any runoff yet; it was all going into the ground, and a rodeo gal couldn't tell where it would run when it did.

She trudged up the road, looking for the second break, and she wasn't going to cry. But then she heard a car motor far down, at the turnoff from the highway, and it could only be Lonnie and she was so glad about it that a couple of tears did start. But she messed them around on her face with the rain water and the sweat and the general accumulation of the day, and there was no way old Lon'd be able to tell that she'd been acting like a pantywaist.

136

But it wasn't Lon. It was Tommy and Dot, in his pickup, with Betsy and Belle standing in the back, tied to a stockframe. Tommy got out and said, "The old barn down at the station leaks so bad I didn't want to put your horses in it, and they oughtn't to stand in a corral; weather bureau says a three-day rain."

She said, "Thanks for bringing them up."

"Well, we borrowed them," Tommy said. Behind him Dot sat dry and happy on the leather seat of the government car. The windshield wiper went back and forth in front of her, and she was wearing a slicker and one of Tommy's old hats, with a broad green ribbon around it. "Lonnie home yet?"

Vera Mae stared at him. "Hell, no," she said. "Don't you know where he is? You borrowed him."

Tommy said, "He and Mark are old enough hands to know fire season's over; they won't hurry to turn their pickup back in. Way I got it, they parked her down at the airport; the fire'll give them bus tickets to the airport, and they'll undoubtedly come right here." He had on a long waterproof coat with a sheepskin collar; he pulled this tighter around his neck and said, "All right if I turn the mares loose here? They'll go right home. These dirt roads get slicker than glass until the real rain washes the top dust off."

Vera Mae said, "I haven't got time to help you unload. I'm trying to get our water breaks open."

Tommy said, "Well, I could put the chains on and drive clear in."

Vera Mae said, "Don't bother. With me here at the gate, they'll have to go home; I can shoo them ahead of me when I walk back."

"All right," the ranger said. "There's a cut bank right ahead here when we can unload."

Vera Mae was careful to stand on the left side of the road, on Tommy's side, so she wouldn't have to say hello to Dot when the lady was driven past her; she had never felt so dirty and ugly in her life. There wasn't really any mud yet, and a little more dirt could hardly have been noticed, but the slight spatter on her boots and pant legs annoyed her. She had shifted to the right side of the road by the time the pickup came by empty.

Tommy stopped. "I could take Dot home and maybe send somebody back to help you."

"No, thanks," Vera Mae said. "I've been buttoning up my own drawers long enough."

He said, "Tell Lonnie I sent Andy Anderson up to the spike camp to break up; any of Lonnie's gear'll be safe in Mark's room till he comes and gets it. We sure had a good fire season; we didn't lose a quarter-section all told."

"That's fine," Vera Mae said. She added, "You can leave the gate open; the kids are up the canyon moving the cows. They'll close it. That way Mrs. Burns won't have to get out in the mud."

Tommy's face got red. He said, "Well, thanks. I wish—" He sat there, saying nothing, his hands on the wheel of the car, the windshield wiper beating time in front of him. There is something so efficient, so well-maintained, about Government cars in the back country that it is annoying to the owners of private vehicles. Vera Mae felt herself hating the car too. "I wish—"

Then he shrugged and put the car into gear, and again a little spatter of mud came up against Vera Mae's boots and her blue jeans. They were the first pair of boots she'd ever bought with her own money, after she'd left her parents to go off and work with the rodeo; they were cracked across the toes and scuffed beyond polishing. But they were hers.

She went back to digging out water breaks.

Before she'd cleaned the second break, blisters formed on her hands, and one of them broke. The kids came by, their horses' backs gleaming with rain. The children themselves were drenched, despite their slickers; they'd been playing wild horseback games under the dripping branches.

138

She told them to go on up to the meadow and see that all the horses were put into the horse pasture. "Betsy and Belle are loose up there, Tommy brought them home."

"Yipes!" Mike yelled. "Fire season's over! Pop'll be staying home all the time. Yippeeeeee!" He and June clapped their legs to their horses and went off at a gallop; one hoof, she couldn't be sure which, sent a little dollup of mud square into her face. It was the final blow, and she went back to digging out that goddamned break while she cried unashamedly.

Lonnie found her still on the second break. He jumped out of the pickup, while Mark gunned the motor and kept the car standing there; he ran up and put his strong, thick arms around her. His old leather jacket smelled worse of smoke now that it was wet.

"What the hell are you doing?" he asked her.

"What the hell do you think I'm doing?" she asked. "I'm cleaning the hell out of the hellish water breaks."

He half-picked her off the ground with one arm around her, the other hand reaching for the long-handled round-point shovel. "You don't do that, baby," he said. "You wait till there's a little runoff, and then you just take the tip of your shovel and guide the water, and the break cleans itself."

She sobbed, paying no regard to Mark in the car or Lonnie here in the mud with her. "Why didn't you tell me?" she asked, and then, recognizing how silly she was being, she started laughing and wriggled out of Lonnie's arms to stand up and kiss him. He half-shoved her toward the pickup, and when she got in, she kissed Mark too, leaving a blotch of mud on his thin cheek. Mark turned red.

They went up the trail, she sitting in the middle of the seat. Lonnie leaned out the window and stared. "Somebody been ahead of us. Those aren't our tires."

"Tommy," she said. "He brought the mares back. Said thanks for the loan."

Across her Mark and Lonnie exchanged glances. Lon

looked out at where the cut bank was, and she knew he'd seen and properly read the marks; how Tommy had unloaded and driven off, leaving her to put the mares in the pasture, to clean out the water breaks.

Mark said, "They don't teach them how to clean a road in college. Just how to send somebody else to do it."

Vera Mae said, "It was all right. The kids were up moving the cattle to the dry field, you know the one where there isn't any water to drink and you said—"

"I know what I said," Lonnie told her. She'd been so upset with her own troubles before that she hadn't realized he was mad about something; now she sensed that Mark was mad too.

"Well, it was all right," Vera Mae said. "The kids took the mares up. They came along just ten minutes later . . . You better check with me, Lonnie, on what I should have covered. I put tarps over the woodcutting rig and the new plumbing and the hay and the corn, and over—"

"Baby," Lonnie said. "Oh, Jesus Christ, baby."

Mark said, "Take it easy, Lon."

Vera Mae said, "Something happened on the fire, didn't it, boys?"

They came off the road and out on the meadow. Lonnie said, "Yeah. We quit. Well, you might say Mark quit; on account of I was let go anyway, with the end of fire season. I ain't likely to go back next year, though."

Vera Mae said, "You'll probably think better of it before then."

"Maybe so I will, but the Forest Service isn't likely to. I beat up on the supervisor of the forest down there."

Vera Mae said, "Oh . . ." She shook her head. "Me and my big head. I thought Tommy was acting the way he was because I'd been snooty to his snotty wife."

"Naw," Lonnie said. "It was me beatin' up on that brass . . . You might as well know. They bolloxed up the relief crews, and a bunch of the boys was left out on the line for two shifts in a row, no water, no food. Old Tait

140

from Red Rock had a heart attack and croaked, and they wanted we should sign something saying he'd been sick coming to the fire."

"I just took off my badge and threw it in the guy's face," Mark said. "It took Lonnie to hit him . . ." He opened his whipcord jacket and pulled his shirt out so Vera Mae could see where the badge pin had torn the cloth. "All the way home I've been telling Lonnie and myself how the brass can't help it; they've got a tough job to do and not enough money to do it with. But us—the silver-badge boys, the back-country brush monkeys who didn't go to college, who can't get permanent appointments—we're nothing more to them than tools to get the work done."

"Nothing more than a bunch of long-handled round-point shovels," Lonnie said. "Or double-bitted axes."

Mark said, "Tait was fifty years old. He worked hard all his life."

"He never turned down a job," Lonnie said.

CHAPTER XII

THERE WAS some left in the bottle Tommy had brought for a wedding present so long ago. Vera Mae got it out but Mark said, "No, thanks," and Lonnie just sort of pushed the bottle away. And maybe that was the worst of all, because all summer there had been so much talk about how drunk they were going to get when the forest got damped down. She poured herself a straight shot, and left it sitting in front of her.

"How'd the patch come out?" Mark asked.

"Swell," Vera Mae said. "Good. The corn's about gone by, but the tomatoes and string beans are still coming along. And the cabbage is just really getting going. And we got so many turnips it makes me sick just to think of 'em."

"Deer season opens next week," Lonnie said. As though making up his mind after a long struggle, he threw an arm behind him and got two glasses off the sink, and poured himself and Mark each a little of the red liquor. He raised his glass, and Vera Mae and Mark picked up theirs. "We can use the rain," Lonnie said, and they each drank about half the shot. Vera Mae felt it warming her.

She said, "I could use that," and laughed, and then felt silly. All of a sudden she sat up straight and slapped herself across the forehead. "My God, I'm a hell of a woman. Where are my kids?"

They all jumped up. The bottle started to fall and Lonnie caught it with his quick hand. Outside, on the porch, the rain licked at them, and it almost sounded like thunder out; then they knew that the rumbling didn't come from the sky, but from the little saddling corral in front of the barn. Nobody bothered to hunt up a slicker as they tumbled down there.

Bob and Ruby, Betsy, Belle and Sweetie were all surging around the little corral trampling the manure to a muddy pulp, kicking at each other and at nothing, while in his flimsy, saddle-horse stall Prince snorted and surged.

Mike was still on Bob, going around and around, out of control but hanging on, and June was huddled against the rails, crying. Lonnie's legs were longer; he snatched her up. She was crying too hard to make any sense.

Vera Mae ran for the overhang. There was a rope on a hook just outside Prince's stall. The light was bad, what with the rain and the ending of the day, and it was not much of a shot, with those damned mares milling around; but she built up the quickest loop of her life and threw, and the rope settled around Bob's neck like he'd pulled it there with a magnet. Bob was rope-broke; the minute he felt the loop tighten, he stood quiet, like any horse who'd been choked once by a riata, and Vera Mae went hand over hand up the line, slapping the mares away with the loose end.

She put up her arms but Mike was a man and he was Lonnie Verdoux's son; he came out of the saddle on his own strength, and stood, swaying a little, hanging onto Bob's stirrup. It was pretty obvious that he was going to cry soon, and that it was going to kill him; Vera Mae took Bob's reins around her hand and made a big thing of re-coiling the lasso rope so she wouldn't see him.

"When we opened the gate to put Betsy and Belle in, Ruby broke out, an' then all the mares got away, an' Sweetie ran away with June, an' I come after."

"Sure," Vera Mae said. "Could happen to anybody . . . Go in the saddle room and get a bunch of rope halters. I'll lass' 'em one at a time. Your old man was smart to marry a trick roper."

"It was that lousy stud's fault," Mike said. "He was yellin' and a-screamin' at 'em. They didn't mean to be bad."

Vera Mae looked over her shoulder. She didn't think that Lonnie had heard what his son had called his prize stallion. "You get those halters, Mike. Fast as I rope 'em, you put a halter on, an' tie off to a fence post." *Tie off* was Hollywood talk, she thought; around here they said *tie up*. Funny time to be thinking of that.

Her rope licked out and got Betsy square; Mike ran in and slid the halter over the pulled-down head as good as if he was a man grown. Vera Mae planted her boot heels in the mud and called out, "You, Lonnie. Take June in the house! Time like this, a lady needs a man to hold her." There was plenty of light to see Lon's face and June's; Lon wanted to get the baby's clothes off, make sure she hadn't been kicked, and June just plain wanted her father.

Mark said, "Give me some of those halters, Mike."

She stood there, and her rope—muddy and stiff and dirty and slippery—flicked and she got a mare every time for Mike and Mark to halter up and tie. Duke would have

143

been proud of her; considering the state of the riata and the light, it was the roping of her life. And she hadn't exactly rested up before it.

Prince was still trying to make kindling out of his stall. She slipped in with him and put a halter on; she threw a rope over one of the rafters and tied him high. Coming out, she said, "Mark, there's a horse blanket in the saddle room. Put it on Prince . . . Mike, go in the house and get those wet clothes off. Wash down good . . . And if I ever hear you calling Prince lousy or anything else except a hell of a bargain again, I'll take my rope and tan your pants."

At once she was aware of what a small boy he really was; these last days, with Lonnie gone, she'd almost forgotten Mike wasn't more than a baby himself. He looked at her, and he made her the second muddiest person in the back country; just about all of Mike you could see was his eyes and a patch here and there of white cheekbone. But he nodded and said, "Yes, Vera Mae," and two tears cut mud down his face. But she couldn't break down now, though she wanted to sweep him up and kiss him; she'd had it to say.

So she got on Bob and gathered up two of the mares' halter ropes at random and pointed down to the horse pasture at a lope, and to hell with falling in the mud. Bob was a horse and he could look after himself. When the mares didn't want to leave Prince she called them a name she hadn't used for some months and hit them with her rein ends, and they came along.

She let Bob pick his speed coming back for the second pair, and the cowpony thudded, the mud flying out behind him, the rain digging through her clothes so she found out she really hadn't been wet before. She was sort of aware that Mark was lighting the old safety lantern and hanging it outside the saddle-room door when she came up; but she took the two last mares—Ruby and Belle—down to the pasture, and being a reckless fool felt so good that she made a third trip bareback and with just a rope halter on Bob.

She gave him a pat and turned him out. It had been a hell of a day for the horse, and he hadn't seemed to mind at all. He ought to have a warm stall and a mess of oats and a rubdown, but he was going to have to take his chances; he was a mountain horse, and he knew enough to run around and roll and all before he went to sleep under a dripping tree or drank a lot of water.

Gelding or not, he was more man than Prince. But it wasn't enough to be a man, the way the world was.

What she wasn't going to do was cry. She was going to walk the long, muddy path back to the house, and—

But she wasn't. Here came Mark in the government pickup, its beautiful headlights cutting the gloom. She jumped in beside him when he slowed down and opened the right-hand door. He shouted, "If I ever stop, I'll never get started again," and started turning. He was sure right. Even in second, the wheels were slithering; if he went into low they'd dig down. "Courtesy of the United States Forest Service," Mark said, and left the road to run on the grass for more traction.

They didn't exactly ride back to the house; they skated, the car going sidewise about as much as it did forward. Mark stopped gingerly in front of the cabin and said, "I'll have to put the chains on to get out."

"We can put you up tonight," Vera Mae said.

Mark said, "I got my bedroll in the pickup box," and they went into the cabin without saying anything more.

Lonnie was in the kitchen. He had taken his leather jacket off and hung it behind the stove; it steamed with a smoky fragrance. His boots were back there too. He sat at the kitchen table, and the whisky bottle was still out; his mood had changed, he looked like a man who had made friends with the jug.

He said, "They're both alseep. I gave 'em some hot cow with whisky in it. Joan taught me that. I gave it to 'em,

145

and they went right to sleep. I rubbed 'em off good with a towel first. They can wash tomorrow."

Vera Mae said, "Sure. That was smart. Joan had some good ideas." She'd never said the name to him before.

Lonnie raised his head, "Yeah? What were they?" He shoved the bottle over. "Snort up, Mark. Your teeth are chattering."

Vera Mae said, "Take your boots off too, Mark. Lady Astorbilt isn't likely to drop in."

Mark said weakly, "I oughta get the pickup back," and then maybe he remembered that the Forest Service couldn't do any more to him than it had done, because he sat down and took off his laced boots and threw them with Lonnie's to dry. He poured hot water from the kettle on some whisky and threw in a little sugar and stirred it with the spoon from the sugar bowl; then he took a sip, and made a face, like he'd burned his mouth.

"That looks like a good idea," Vera Mae said, and made herself a hot toddy.

They sat there an awful long time, and nobody seemed to have much to say. It was good dark now, and this seemed to encourage the rain and the wind; there was plenty of noise without anybody saying anything. Finally, Lonnie said, "Tomorrow, if it lets up a little, I'll bring in the wood stove."

Vera Mae said, "Look, Lonnie, I'm sorry if I let the kids work too hard."

Lonnie raised his head. "Who's griping? You done good. They had it to do, to help you, and there's nothing wrong with them some sleep won't heal up and hair over. If you're sore about me sayin' it was Joan's idea to put whisky in their milk, forget it. Joan's dead, and that's all there is to it."

Vera Mae said, "But—"

Lonnie brought his hand down on the table. "What'd Mike mean calling Prince a lousy stud? He didn't make that up, he heard it from you. Just because he hasn't

146

caught the mares, because they're still horsing—whata you expect, he's only been here two weeks. And it ain't the best time of year to breed a mare."

"Mike didn't mean anything," Vera Mae said. "He's just a kid. And it isn't Prince's fault the mares are horsing. I haven't left them with him."

"Because he isn't any good? Because he doesn't have a bunch of fancy pants rodeo ribbons and silver cups?"

"Because," Vera Mae said, "it isn't the right time of year. You said it, yourself."

Lon's voice rattled the glasses on the sink. "In this country, you can raise early fall colts as easy as not! You know it. There ain't a damn thing about a horse you don't know. You sore because I picked him out? Because I didn't run to you for advice?"

Mark half-rose from his chair. Then he sat back again. Vera Mae had time to be sorry for him, pinched in the middle of a family fight, but her temper was slipping too fast for her to be sorry for anybody. "You and Mike and your good pal Tommy are always talking about the grass," she said. "Like you counted every blade on the place. Well, I didn't want to see your precious goddamned grass get trampled down by a bunch of lousy two-bit colts."

Lonnie set his drink down with a crash. "What kind of dude nonsense you talking? There ain't nothing heredity in those bad legs of his, and outside of that he's as good a horse as a man could ask for. Maybe you got big ideas from hanging around your Hollywood pals and your—"

Any hold she'd had on her temper went right then. "You talked awful big when I first met you about your Mulemouth stud! You didn't mention any stove-up, gimp-legged Steeldusts that some pinch-penny rich man threw away!"

"Who throwed what away?" Lonnie asked. "I worked my seat off to buy that Prince for you! An' I never said I had Mulemouth! Said I had had him, an' he got away!"

There was a wooden box under the sink, half-full of

flattened-out tin cans to be buried. Lonnie took his glass and threw it at this box, and it broke on the wall above the box; most of the pieces fell in.

At once June's voice was heard, in the bedroom. She yelled, "Mommie!" once. She'd never called Vera Mae that, or mother, or anything but Vera Mae.

Vera Mae jumped up and crossed the hall and opened the bedroom door. They were both asleep, June's face twisted up, but her eyes closed. She knelt by the bed and took a corner of the sheet and wiped sweat off June's forehead. The wrinkles came out and the little girl slid down into some deeper and more comfortable level of sleep.

Vera Mae took time to stand in front of the bedroom mirror and powder her nose, put on lipstick. She noticed she was still dirty up under the hairline, but the light wasn't very good in the kitchen. She went back there and stood in the door, and said, "I'm sorry, Lon. And to you, Mark, for letting you into the middle of this. I guess I kind of had a busy day."

Lonnie got up and got a fresh glass. He filled a pitcher of water, and put it on the table, and mixed them three highballs. "Too bad the bottle's so far down, and us so far from a package store," he said . . . "Vera Mae, what's wrong with Prince?"

She picked up her glass and smiled over it at the two men. "Lonnie, I told you when I married you, what goes on inside this house is my business, and you run the ranch. That still goes."

He shook his head. "I'm not sore now. You're a better horseman than I am and always have been. Even if you used to think the way to move a cow was to shoot off a gun and have Roy Rogers sing a song to him."

She hesitated. But his eyes were quiet and calm, and she knew from June's single outcry an awful lot she hadn't known before; that Joan had tormented him, that when he'd lived with Joan he'd had a lousy temper, that he and the kids both were so glad she'd taken Joan's place that

148

nothing she could do or say would ever make them really mad at her.

So she let him have it. She said, "A colt's worth five dollars or ten dollars or a sock in the head so you don't have him around when you want to work his mother. And a yearling's worth no more. You have to feed a horse till he's three years old to sell him. And, by that time, you could have used his feed to turn out a couple of tons of beef. That right?"

Lonnie said, "I'll let Mark do the multiplyin'. But roughly, yeah. So what? A good horse—"

"Is worth a lot of money," Vera Mae said. "If you can sell him. And the only way you can sell him as a yearling, or even a green-broke two-year-old is because people know who his papa was . . . And as a three-year-old, the only way you can sell him for more than fifty bucks is either he works wonderful and people see him doing it, or he comes from a stud that got a lot of blue ribbons and stuff, and then people'll drive their cars from clear back in Colorado. And whoever heard of Prince?"

Lonnie said, "If this makes sense to you, Mark, just tell me. Who in God's name ever heard of Mulemouth, fifty miles away?"

"Mulemouth could be broke," Vera Mae said. "He could be trained. With all you know and all I know, he could learn to do more than any other horse in the business. Being tougher, and all. And people would like the part about him being on the desert on his own till he was full-growed. We coulda taken him to the State Fair, maybe send him on the circuit with Duke, or taken him ourself. Prince, he's done for. You got Old Man Trellis's word he used to amount to something."

She finished. There was a lot more she could have said, but she felt sick. She couldn't look at Lonnie. If it hadn't happened in front of Mark, maybe it would have been all right, but it had.

And there never was a man in the world could have a

woman tell him his business in front of another man, and not either turn into a weak sister or blow his top.

Except—and as she raised her head she knew it—except Lonnie Verdoux.

He slowly grinned, just like he hadn't been on a fire for two weeks, just like he hadn't had a hell of a day, just like his wife hadn't just taken the pants away from him—and he said, "Well, I told you when I married you I was a dumb son. Why didn't I think of that?"

He reached out and sweetened their drinks. "No use keeping a nasty little stub of liquor like that around," he said. "Jesus, Mark, how did I ever catch Vera Mae?"

Mark Somers spoke for the first time in an awful long time. "Just born lucky," he said. "Look, Lonnie, we'll get up a gang. Stan Trellis, and some of the boys from over on the reservation and maybe a bunch of town guys, I know some of them. Come spring, we'll all turn out and help you catch Mulemouth. Soon as the winter rains have sweetened up the alkali ponds."

"I take that kindly," Lonnie said. "Don't you, Vera Mae? Yeah, I can see it now. With my only cash job gone, and a big feed bill to carry a stud I can't use, I'll sure'n hell need old Mulemouth back. Maybe so if we had us a posse of—say, a hundred men, we could get him, sure enough."

Vera Mae said, "Maybe Old Man Trellis'd take Prince back, as a gift."

Lonnie stood up and finished his drink standing. "Sure. Worth lookin' into. I'm gonna cork off. Mark, you need any help?"

"I'll get on back to the station," Mark said. "The rain'll have washed the top slick off the road, I can make it out."

"Bring your bedroll in here," Lonnie said. "I'll help you."

"I'll think of you when I'm taking a hot bath," Mark said, and left.

Lonnie stared after him until the car motor roared. Then

he went to the door. "Started okay," he said. Outside, the rain splashed off the roof.

"In Hollywood, when it rained," Vera Mae said, "we used to put buckets under the rainspouts, catch the water to wash our hair in. But our water on the ranch is sure soft."

"Yeah," Lonnie said absently. He squinted into the night. "He made it over the rise," he said. "It's all downhill from there." He came back in, stretching, rubbing spray from the open door around on his face. "You're a good girl, Vera Mae."

She jumped up and stood in front of him. "Lonnie, it'll be all right! We got it good! We've hardly touched your salary, and it's almost time to beef out the herd, and cow prices have held up and—"

"And as long as they do," Lonnie said, "we make a thousand dollars a year."

"Yes," she said, "but rent free. And our vegetables, and corn and the pigs for bacon and ham; deer season opening up and we'll can some meat from it, I heard how once and—"

"Twenty lousy dollars a week," Lonnie said. "With beef at twenty-five dollars a hundred. It went to three dollars once, and if it did again, we'd be making a handful of change a month . . . before taxes."

She said, "If I went back on the rodeo—"

His harsh "No" cut her off. "I'll crawl on my belly to Tommy, and maybe he'll take me back next year . . . Or maybe it isn't like I always heard, and a man fired from one Civil Service job isn't barred out of another . . . Wentworth up at the Fish Hatchery always liked me, and Joe at the State Highway Maintenance . . ."

"All right," she said. One of the lamps started to flicker, and she turned it off. "I forgot to fill the lamps. All right. If you get a job, I'll crawl to your boss's wife this time. I mean it the right way, Lonnie! I coulda said yes Dot and no Dot, and maybe—"

"It's got nothing to do with it," Lonnie said. "What I'm wondering is, if I'da been as brash with that supervisor without a stud horse to back me up. If I was saying to myself, I'm a horsebreeder now, not a tin-badge brush monkey. If I was saying, I've always hated it taking it off you brass, and now I'm through."

"I thought you liked the Forest Service," Vera Mae said.

Lonnie said, "Sure. Oh, yeah. It's good work. If I'd gone to college, or maybe even if I'd never thought of anything better. But nobody likes working for wages," he said. "And I thought when I had Mulemouth and again when I had Prince . . . I'm dumb, Vera Mae."

"You're worn out," she said. "Go to bed. We'll think of something. We could raise chickens or rabbits or—"

"Sure," he said. His grin was almost Lonnie Verdoux's grin. "We could raise mushrooms in the cellar, if we had a cellar . . . You talk good sense some of the time, like when you told me to go to bed. We don't have to even worry till spring, we weren't looking for no more outside money till then."

He half-raised a hand from which he hadn't washed off all the grime, and turned into the bedroom. By the time she had turned out the lamps and put the glasses into the sink, he was asleep. She dropped her own clothes on the floor, and crawled in, and never remembered a thing.

And when she woke up in the morning, he was gone. At first she thought he was feeding Prince or maybe hauling hay down to the pasture.

But Prince was gone, and so was Lonnie's saddle, and so were her two best ropes.

It was still raining, and it was a steady rain that wiped out tracks as fast as you made them.

Then her heart was as cold as the rain until she ran back into the house and opened the other bedroom door. But Mike's head was on one pillow and June's on the other, and they were still asleep, tricked by the cold gray light into thinking it was still early.

152

She could saddle a horse and go down to the station, see Mark, he was still their friend. But she could hear Mark saying, "Lonnie Verdoux wouldn't go off and leave his kids."

And she could add to that he'd never go off and leave her, either.

So . . .

He had said, "If we had a hundred men and we waited for spring—"

But he wouldn't have been Lonnie Verdoux if he'd let her worry till spring, their money running down and nothing ahead.

He wouldn't have been Lonnie Verdoux if he'd even waited till he was good rested from the fire. Not him. A couple of hours sleep, and take off in the rain after Mulemouth.

And there was only one thing to do, no matter how much she wanted to ride after him and help him. The one thing was to stay here and see his house and his kids were looking good when he got back.

Let him go. He'd had it to do, hadn't he?

PART THREE

THE DESERT

CHAPTER I

WHAT HAD BEEN a bad rain on the homestead thinned out to a drizzle on the ridge. Where the updraft came boiling up, it was still wet, and colder than hell, but the dampness wouldn't stick; it seemed to go up in steam as fast as it hit you. Old Prince started moving out, and everything Old Man Trellis had said about him was right; he'd been a lot of horse in his day.

Then the twisting downgrade started, not brushy, but covered with rocks that rolled and twisted under Prince's feet. On every switchback the stud threw his hips wide, wearing himself out.

By eight in the morning they were halfway down to the desert. Lonnie stopped and tied a burlap nosebag full of barley on Prince's nose; then he took a set of bronc shoes and a hammer, file and nippers from his saddle bags, and shod the stallion as best he could. He hadn't dared to do the job at the ranch, where he could have burned good shoes on; the noise would have waked the folks.

He ate some dried raisins, and when he shoved along, he left his smithing tools under a rock by the trail. He'd brought only one set of shoes with him. This wasn't like the other time he'd come after Mulemouth; Prince wouldn't last through the four sets of shoes that Bob had worn out.

Noon was hot, and they were on the desert floor, and his fears about Prince were pretty much over; the old boy had made it down, which was what Lonnie had worried about most. The rest of it—Prince's lack of endurance, the

154

light bait of food Lonnie was carrying—they weren't worries; they were for certain. He either got Mulemouth fast, or he didn't get him at all, and that was a fact.

He set out across the desert for what used to be the buckskin stud's ranging ground. The signs were kind of favorable. Desert verbena and bunch grass were coming up, and there was a sort of green scum over the desert when it got a ways from you. It had rained pretty recent, the alkali lakes wouldn't be as bad as they'd been through the summer; man'd get kind of sick, maybe, but an old brush-whicker like Lonnie could keep going.

Prince might have a little trouble because, while he'd lived right near to the rim of the desert all his life, Prince had been kind of protected from such rough things as missing a meal and sleeping out in the cold and drinking bitter water. If Prince came through, he'd sure take care of him good the rest of his life, though it'd be hard work, having two studs on the ranch.

Maybe he could use Prince for breeding to Mulemouth's daughters. If he got Mulemouth. If Prince came through. If he . . .

Antelope had been through here; he saw their droppings and the close cropping they'd given the bunch grass. He rode through the mesquite grove and scattered a herd of wild burros. The stud turned and wheeled, rearing at Prince; Prince trumpeted back, but Lonnie at once turned his horse away from the burro mares, and their stud took them off at an angle from Prince's path.

Old Prince snorted after them wistfully. Maybe he could keep Prince and catch him a bunch of burro mares and raise mules. Maybe he could fly too.

The shadow of the first butte, the shimmer of the first alkali lake lay ahead of him; the afternoon was running out. Prince still walked easy, the old boy was stiff but game; Lonnie had a little twinge of conscience at what he was doing, but just a little one. Horses were made for men to use, though the fool women that used to fuss over him when he was traveling rodeo had sometimes indicated that a man's proudest job would be chambermaiding one of the animals; he'd never seen it that way.

He was pretty far into wild horse country now, though he'd cut no sign. He swung down by the edge of the alkali lake and took Prince's saddle off. He slipped the bridle down for a halter and led the stud over the crackling white alkali to the edge of the lake.

Prince didn't act eager. It was no trouble to hold him back with one hand and lower the canteen by its cover chain with the other. When the canteen was full, Lonnie slackened his hold on the reins, and the stallion lowered his veteran head and blew at the water.

He blew quite a while, and then he raised his head again. Lonnie shrugged. He'd drink in the morning; he'd have to learn to. He rigged a hackamore and picket line out of one of the lass' ropes, and thanked the Lord that Vera Mae wasn't there to watch him do it, and her a trick roper.

He tied one end of the rope to his saddle and leaned back against the fork with his carbine, watching the water hole. Thirty caliber was kind of heavy for blowing the head off a desert quail, which was what he hoped to do, but he hadn't wanted to drag a gun under each leg . . .

Misusing her riata had brought Vera Mae to mind, and he began to feel bad, with what he realized must be loneliness. It made his stomach ache, so he couldn't help thinking about steaks and hot coffee and biscuits with milk gravy. It made his throat dry for a bottle of beer, or maybe some whisky and sugar and water.

So this is being lonely, he thought. Just like being hungry or thirsty is all. Funny, and they write all those songs about it. Don't write any about missing a square meal. Well, there's "Cool Water." Pretty rough down there in the South, Southern Cal., Arizona, Nevada, man must get awful thirsty. Up here you can always get a drink, even if it ain't always appetizing.

He glanced over at Prince. The horse wasn't so bad off

156

he wasn't cropping at the bunch grass. Make a real desert rat out of Old Man Trellis's pet stud; by tomorrow he'd be chewing mesquite beans and liking 'em . . . Old Man Trellis was hell on his family, but he was sure good to his stock.

About now Vera Mae'd be calling the kids in and checking to see they did their homework before it was time to wash up for dinner. Maybe she'd take her boots off and be paddling around the kitchen in her stocking feet; she did that sometimes and it sure made her look small. Seeing her in her boots all day, you thought of her as a tall sort of girl, and then she crossed you up by taking them off, and she was just about right to pick up and hold a while.

Living with a girl like that, a man'd never get tired. He just had to see she had what she wanted to make her happy. And she wasn't demanding, God knows. Now, Joan was a cheap feed all right, never asked for anything, and where was the fun in that? You got her something, and she didn't like it; you didn't get her something, and she didn't like that either.

Vera Mae, she didn't nag for little things, but when she wanted something, you better go get it, and now, because you knew she'd thought it over, and it was the thing to get . . .

He wished he'd borrowed Vera Mae's little 16-gauge shotgun. But if you didn't run into something, a carbine was safer; you could always shoot you an antelope or a burro with it. Lot worse meat than wild jackass. And it would be irritating to be carrying a 16-gauge, and starve to death right in front of something that a big gun would bring down.

He glanced at the butte. The shadow was pulling out about as far as it would go, and no quail had come to water. Pretty soon it would be too dark to hit a quail, anyway, without blowing it to pieces.

Overhead a V of ducks faltered, heading south. Ducks'd be landing on the alkali pond pretty soon for the night, but the man didn't live could hit a duck with a .30-06. So Lonnie Verdoux shot a jackrabbit.

He skinned it and gutted it, and built a fire of tules and mesquite branches and buried his jackrabbit. He'd dig it up in a couple of hours from being buried on the coals, and it would be done enough to let him bite the meat off the legs and ribs.

But it wouldn't taste any better than any other jackrabbit ever had, and that was not good.

He took a slug of water from the canteen, and that wasn't too good either. The noise of the gun had hardly bothered Prince, but the canteen chain rattling brought his head up. Lonnie swiveled around, but that's all it was. He'd give a nickel to hear the old boy whistle once or trumpet.

But if he did, it would probably just be a herd of wild burros.

Lonnie rested back on the saddle and went to sleep till his jackrabbit barbecue was—in a manner of speaking—ready to eat.

CHAPTER II

THREE TIMES during the night Lonnie moved, giving Prince fresh bunch grass to gnaw at. It wouldn't keep the big fellow from gaunting, but it would put off his complete breakdown by maybe a day. Just like the saddle blanket Lonnie wrapped in wouldn't keep him from freezing; it'd just draw out the process.

At false dawn he got up and put the blanket back on Prince, threw the saddle on top and cinched it loose. He left the bridle on its watering hooks and trudged back to the alkali pond. This time Prince didn't blow quite so long, and if he didn't drink, he at least washed out his mouth a little.

About half the jackrabbit was left. Lonnie wrapped a hind leg in the wax paper from around the raisin box, and gnawed on the front leg as he rode along.

He hadn't put the bit back into Prince's mouth; he'd let the stud graze as he went. He dallied the reins around the horn, and sat easy in the saddle; after he'd wiped burnt jackrabbit from his mouth with the sleeve of his fire jacket, he rolled a cigarette. It tasted awful. He wished he'd remembered to steal some coffee when he took off from the ranch.

Next time he shot something to bake, he'd try and roast a handful of Prince's barley, you could make coffee out of that.

Lord, he hadn't thought about that trick in a long time. Not since 1933, when his father'd gotten a job as foreman with a WPA crew that was building rock culverts on the highway, gotten a job and brought some real coffee home with the first government check.

Lonnie'd not had so much coffee in his life that whether it really had coffee in it or not made any difference to him. He was riding for Old Man Trellis winters then and doing what he could do in the summer . . .

Old Man Trellis had been real kindly to give him the job, and him just over being thirteen, just a droop-nosed kid. It had been kind of a good job, too, no boss; Lonnie and Ben Davis, who was thirty but no brighter than a kid of ten, would ride into Squawberry Valley just before Christmas and batch it through the snow in Old Man Trellis's log-and-tinroof line cabin up there. Whenever the snow got deep, they'd go out on snowshoes, tailing up the cattle that got bogged down; whenever the cold got bad they'd chop the ice so the cows could drink easy. Squawberry Valley was full of oak trees that a steer could browse when he couldn't paw down for grass, and the cows used to fatten nice in the worst years.

159

He'd learned a lot about a cow back there, on account of there wasn't much to do but watch the beef; nothing Ben Davis said after the first day was likely to hold even a kid's interest, on account of Ben Davis said the same things every day.

It was sure all right of Old Man to give him the job. Fifteen dollars a month, and groceries—dried prunes and raisins, spuds, flour, salt and pepper, and a side of bacon for each man. It was all they needed, and they ate long-legged rabbit till Lonnie hardly ever went deer hunting again. One thing about Squawberry in winter that you could count on was that there was no game warden likely to drop in. A man was his own boss, and Ben Davis's boss too.

Thinking back like this made him feel better, and the second cigarette tasted all right. Maybe he shouldn't be smoking, smells carried a long distance on the desert, but he wasn't trying to sneak up on Mulemouth. That was the way he'd gotten the buckskin last time, but it took too long and all. Besides, that was for spring; any ranch horse you brought down here this time of year was probably not going back, and he wasn't going to lose Vera Mae's mares, nor yet Bob.

He felt bad about what he was doing to Prince and tried not to think of it, and just to cross him up, Prince called attention to himself now. He raised his head and whistled, clear and loud, and his stiff hind legs started limbering up. He even reared about six inches and beat at the ground with his front hoofs.

Lonnie slipped down and put the bit in Prince's mouth; he was pleased that the old boy felt good enough to fight him about it. When Lonnie got back in the saddle he un-coiled the rope that he'd used for a tie last night, and dragged it to unkink it. It was a real linen rope that was Vera Mae's; cost probably as much as everything he wore, including boots and hat.

Prince was heading for a little old butte off to the

southeast; he let him go. Horses, especially tame ones, don't have a good sense of smell like a dog, but they can hear an awful long distance; longer than any man, even the best Indian tracker . . .

Prince struck out across the desert, and he moved right out.

Yeah, if he missed coffee, he had Mr. Roosevelt to thank. He'd learned to drink it when his dad got on the WPA, and later on he'd gotten so he couldn't start the day without it. This was when he got old enough himself to get in the CCC. That was where he'd made so many Indian acquaintances, because at first he'd been the only white boy around there enrolling, and they'd put him in an Indian camp, over on the reservation.

They'd built water troughs all over that reservation, marking each one CCC-ID, for Indian Division, and Johnny Taylow, his best Indian pal, had scratched under that, before the cement could harden: + L. Verdoux. They'd kidded him a lot, those Indian boys, always threatening to scalp him, and calling him a fisheater because he called sardines sardines instead of lizards, and salmon salmon instead of rattlesnake meat. But they were all right to work with, holding up their own end and making jokes so the day didn't seem so long, and he'd been kind of homesick when a camp of white boys opened up and he was transferred.

The white boys were city boys, and a lot tougher than he'd care to ever be. All they could talk about was stealing cars and doing things with girls he'd never done yet, and him married twice and traveled around after rodeos a year to boot. And the work hadn't been as good, building fireplaces in public camps that were never likely to be used unless the ocean came up and flooded out all the cities and everybody moved back on the national forests.

Lonnie sat easy in the saddle, letting old Prince line out across the desert. The stud wanted to run, but he held him down.

Hell, he had no fight with the CCC's. If it hadn't been for them, he'd never have gotten his high-school diploma; he got it in C schools, and they paid better, even for building fireplaces that'd never be used, than Old Man Trellis had for tailing up nine-hundred-pound steers. But then beef had only been three dollars a hundred, and nobody was paying nothing for riders.

Prince was fighting the bit like he still had rings on his teeth. Lonnie settled down in the saddle, and when the cowhorse decided he couldn't lope, he went into a trot that really covered country, and also shook Lonnie up considerable.

Then the feel of the lines told Lonnie they were getting where Prince wanted to go, and he stood in the saddle, looking over the butte; almost always the wild studs got up there where they could look out a distance. But he didn't see any kind of bump or movement that could be a horse anyplace. He wished now he hadn't smoked, because maybe then he would be able to smell the herd; the wind was toward him.

Then Prince was stopping, and Lonnie slid down to slip the bridle again. Because what the old boy had been lining for was not a stallion to fight or a mare to breed but just a pool of good water trapped in a little sandstone basin.

Lonnie dumped his canteen, and drank and filled it, and Prince was right, it was the purest rain water and not a trace of alkali in it. While the stud filled up too, Lonnie loosened his belt and felt the good feeling of a bellyful of clean liquid. He ate some raisins, and thanked his horse for finding the water, anyway.

It wasn't Prince's fault that he'd belonged to an old mossback like Old Man Trellis, and so didn't have anything to show for what a good horse he'd been. If Lonnie'd gone on riding Squawberry Valley, Old Man would have taken him on steady and then nobody would ever know that Lon Verdoux was educated, no matter how many books he'd managed to borrow from Stan, who went

162

to school in town every day. It was Lon's good luck he'd gone into the CCC's, and Prince's bad luck he hadn't been entered in a lot of horse shows and fairs and rodeos, so one of them had a paper to show and the other didn't.

He put the bit back in Prince's mouth and fought the horse away from his water hole; rode him into the wind three or four miles, and then fixed him to graze and walk again. There was a lot of strength in Prince's neck still, and it was getting toward midmorning, and Lonnie had worked up a little sweat. He tied the old leather jacket behind the saddle, and thought awhile, and then threw away his tobacco and papers.

If smelling out a herd was what it took, he'd have to do it. This wasn't a time to be pampering yourself.

He thought back over what he'd figured out about his high-school paper and Prince's lack of any kind of papers at all. That wasn't bad thinking for a dumb fellow. Maybe if he'd known then what he knew now, he'd have stuck it out with those tough C kids, instead of running away to work rodeo with old Wheelwright.

That way, maybe he would have heard about some way Mr. Roosevelt could fix it so a mountain boy could get to college and get a real paper, like Tommy had. If that had happened, he would have been a brass in the Forest Service, instead of a monkey on the end of a shovel, and he would have drawn wages the whole year around and had a nice government house to bring a wife to.

But it hadn't, and it would be a poor kind of man who wouldn't remember Mr. Roosevelt kindly for what help he'd gotten. Back there in '32 it had sure looked like he and the rest of the Verdoux were going to have to forget about eating for a spell.

Three-dollar beef, and the state so hard up they'd put the game wardens on a sort of share basis, so that a man didn't dare knock himself off a piece of meat out of season. The dungarees the C's had issued him had been the first

163

pair of pants in an awful long time that reached his boot tops.

The store at Salal Flats had gone bust and closed, and the tires had worn clear off their Model T, and it was one long trek into the town on a horse, and no credit when you got there. The sheriff had taken away the ranch his dad had bought after the first World War and would have taken the homestead too, but you can't take a homestead away from a man. Have to leave him that and his gun and his plough and a few cows and a horse for each member of the family, and some other stuff. Only it would have been a good thing if they'd taken his dad's plough before he ever put it to breaking up the grass on the homestead.

Prince was showing no mind to go anyplace at all, and Lonnie put his own mind on it. After the first fall rain now, the grass would be coming up in the draws, and it was likely to be mighty tempting to a band of horses that hadn't tasted green for three, four months. If he could spot a draw. The desert floor was so flat you could pass within a mile of something the size of the Grand Canyon and never know it was there. If he'd had Bob or Betsy, or one of the sorrels, he'd have climbed a butte for a look-see, but he doubted if Prince'd be able to get back down once he got up. Horse with stiff legs was sure hell coming down-hill.

He shut his eyes, thinking back how the desert looked from up on the rim. He'd been there plenty in his life, looking out. As a damn-fool kid, he used to ride up there and dream about catching him a wild horse like—well, like Mulemouth. But it was only three, four years ago that the prospectors and antelope hunters had begun to spread the rumor about the buckskin stud. Then it was Lonnie first took the chance and went after him.

Bet that hurt Old Man Trellis, all that money running wild and somebody else getting it. Bet it pleased him when Mulemouth got away on Jo—on Lonnie.

From the rim you could see the big butte where he'd

164

camped the night before, and then the little butte where Prince had found the sweet water, and then—yeah—over that way there was a crease and—

Golly, yeah, that was a good deep draw in there. If there was a way down into it that wouldn't throw Prince for a crippling loss.

He swung the reins that way and headed for the head of the draw, where it would take off gradual into the fall below the desert floor. Prince wasn't any too favorable about this direction, which was away from home and from the sandstone water basin, too, but Lonnie was wearing spurs.

At noon he began to pick up antelope tracks and wild burro tracks, and then, cutting in from the south, some horse tracks too. It was hard not to swing his legs and make the old devil move out, but there wasn't any hurry. Chances were about five to one that it was not Mulemouth's band that had gone down to the draw.

But—another thing he mustn't do is sing. Passed the time, but it burnt up water and it made a man-noise, and those were the two things he couldn't do. The wind was in his favor, what there was of it, and he could have smoked if he'd not been so sort of final about throwing his makings away. But he could say the words to a song under his breath, and maybe that would pass the time . . .

At two in the afternoon he was getting far enough into the draw to pick a trail through the shade on the west side. Tracks were heavy in here, for the desert; plenty of them were horse tracks too, but none of them of any great size. It didn't necessarily signify that Mulemouth wasn't ahead of him; his other trip after the wild horse had taught him that studs more often led their bands than trailed after them. The small hoofs of the mares could have wiped over his big well-shaped ones.

There was chance and chance again to shoot an antelope. But there was a lot against it, and only a full belly for it; he didn't want his stud to smell of pronghorn blood, he

165

wanted him to smell like a stud; he didn't want a gunshot rioting everything in sight. Not unless this was a box canyon he was riding into . . .

Now he began to see the animals, and Prince began to see good fresh grass. But he kept the stud bitted up; tame horse like Prince—and especially one smooth-mouthed from age—couldn't get any good at all out of that sprouted grass, thin and short as hair on a baby's head.

Antelope charged past him, getting out of that draw that he might trap them in. Too bad about scaring them away from their meal, but they'd come back behind him. And there was a mare, standing head down, drooping, a little old wet colt nuzzling at her. Grulla mare and a pinto colt; no indication of anything. She didn't look up as he went by.

Most wild horses were pintos, and Tommy'd given a real interesting talk about it one time, when they were all lying around, waiting to be called for a fire over in Red Rock Ranger District. Tommy'd said the professors figured all horses had been pinto once, but men had picked them over for size and color and cut the rest for geldings or left them wild, and so when horses got away and bred back to what they used to be you had something like Shetland ponies. Only with big heads and big paunches to hold their feed when they had to run for it.

Lot of grullas in the desert, too, but Tommy hadn't known where the mouse color came from. Take a grulla with striped hoofs, and you had you a horse that you might just as well let run bare; hoofs were tough as iron.

Tommy knew an awful lot, and he was a pretty nice fellow. It was too bad the way it had all turned out. All you could say about the brass in the Forest Service was that they had it to do. He didn't want to criticize Vera Mae, but she couldn't see how fellows like Tommy had an awful lot to protect; all those years in college and as assistant rangers before they got a real appointment; and by that time they were too old to quit and maybe become

166

doctors or lawyers or something; they had to do what the big brass in Washington told them to do, and the big brass had to do what the Secretary of Agriculture told them to, and the Secretary had to do what Congress gave him money to do. And for some damn reason, Congress never gave him enough money, and something was always breaking—usually the guards, like Lonnie, like poor old Tait.

The way it was, you could not send more than fifteen men out on a fire without a trained crew leader. Otherwise, time had showed, they would probably get hurt. And since money was so short, there never were quite enough silver-badge men to be crew leaders and sector bosses and zone bosses. So somebody had to work overtime.

And it oughtn't to be the brass. If a brush monkey got the callouses burnt off the bottom of his feet, or broke a leg, or ate too much smoke, or any of the other things, why he could go back to ranching or punching cows, ploughing or working in a lumber mill or what not. If a brass got fire-useless, he couldn't do a thing but throw away that expensive college education. The brass wasn't yellow, but it didn't take the long hours on the line that the brush monkeys did.

Some of the fellows—

Prince stopped dead. He bowed his neck, and his ears stood up like they'd been starched, and his front feet came off the ground twice as far as Lonnie'd ever seen them before. Lonnie squinched down in the saddle and felt his ropes to see they were ready to come free.

Prince whistled, and some other stallion answered him, and Lonnie threw his best line free and dragged it till he'd built a good big loop. The draw turned up ahead in a dogleg, and he couldn't see what was coming at him. But it sure was a manly whistle.

He swung his spurs and made Prince go forward at a gallop, and the old horse was agreeable. They went around the dogleg at a dead run, because there was no telling; the wild stud might have spotted that there was a man on

167

Prince and made up his mind to take his mares up over the canyon wall.

But this one hadn't. There he stood, all thirteen hands of him, jug-headed, knot-legged and bald-faced on a dirty pinto-colored body. And he was ready to fight Prince to the death for his band of broomtailed, misshapen mares.

Lonnie pulled the old boy down, and he had to put both hands on the lines to do it, finally had to tug on the romal with his right hand to choke Prince, because he was afraid that the bit would break his jaw.

The little wild stallion stood his ground, his mares huddled behind him and whickering with interest at this strange horse. Prince wasn't scared, you couldn't say that of him. But he was standing straight on to the wild horse, not quartering like he'd do if he'd been in many fights; if that little stud charged and reared, he'd rake Prince's face and head first thing.

Lonnie crouched in the saddle, hanging on with his knees, getting his good rope coiled up again with one hand, and back on the thongs. Then he used both hands and his spurs and his rein ends and just about everything else he owned to pull Prince around.

The big fellow didn't come around easy at best, and now he didn't want to. The old fool wanted that harem full of jug-headed mares.

There was a lot of life in Prince, if not much sense. Even after he'd been horsed around, he stood stiff and unwilling to leave that place.

Lonnie beat on him with everything he had, including the coiled riata, and Prince broke into a lumbering run down the draw. Behind them the jug-head let out a snort and a whistle of triumph; must look like a real big shot to those broomtails of his, running off such a big stallion.

Lonnie calmed Prince down to a walk, and the stud seemed to have forgotten there was anything in the draw he wanted. Sure wasn't anything Lonnie wanted; old Mule-

168

mouth was not the horse to let another stud into any draw he decided to use.

CHAPTER III

THERE WASN'T much left to the day when Lonnie got out of the draw. He looked over toward the rimrock that was so close to where he owned; the rain clouds were gone, and it wouldn't be too tough on the ranch for Vera Mae.

There wasn't much left to Prince, either. Lonnie thought of the Forest Service phrase for a poor man; a hot fire and a cold breakfast'd kill him. Sometimes they said it to mean a woman instead of a fire. That was old Prince.

Lonnie turned the old tired head south, away from home. But Prince had forgotten which way home was; he didn't fight. His feet dragged, and once he tripped over a down branch of yucca stalk that shouldn't bother a saddle mouse.

It was better with your back to the ranch. No use thinking about that till you were ready to head that way. Just let Prince amble another hour or so, maybe he'll find water he doesn't mind drinking.

Think about the Forest Service, 'cause you're never heading that way any more. He'd fought lots of fire in his summers in the CCC's, and counting those you could say he'd only missed one summer since he was sixteen. And even as a kid, he'd been pickup labor on some smokes . . . long enough. He'd fought fire longer than any other brush monkey on the Forest. Longer than any of the particular brass around here, either; even the supervisor was only ten years out of college.

So next year if he wanted cash, maybe he could get on the highway. But Vera Mae wouldn't like that either. He could see how it was with her. When he'd been traveling around, he'd landed in a hospital once, result of misjudging the pitching powers of a Brahma bull, and he remembered how he'd felt about the orderlies, guys in white coats just like the doctors, but never going to get any higher than carrying bedpans and moving the heavy patients.

That was how it was if you worked for an outfit where the top men had all gone to college and you hadn't. Only a dumb man like Lonnie would have taken so long to figure that out, and then not till Vera Mae brought it home to him . . .

Clint Clinto in the SCS was a college man, so was Joe Howard on the highway; and Wentworth at the hatchery. There weren't any other jobs around here, unless he went back to working for Old Man, so Vera Mae was right, and—

Everything he thought about turned back to Vera Mae, and that made him feel bad. But you couldn't ride and not think. Not unless you were like Ben Davis. Ben was in jail someplace, he'd heard, scared a girl and they called it rape. Too bad, because there wasn't any real harm in Ben, but there wasn't much good, either; just nothing. Still and all, in the old days he'd felt good when Ben had bellied up to the table and rubbed his hands together because Lonnie'd fixed biscuits and milk gravy.

But hell, he'd been a kid then, and Ben Davis was the first man he'd met who was dumb enough to like Lonnie's cooking. That was all. Ben was probably rubbing his hands right now over what the prison cooks put in front of him. And it was natural that Ben'd get in trouble over girls, on account of there wasn't one anyplace that'd go with him willing . . .

Even at thirteen, though, Lonnie'd been able to manage him, and if he ever got the ranch going good, he'd get somebody like Stan or Clint or Tommy to see about parol-

170

ing Ben to him. Be a sight to see the old boy when he got a chance at Vera Mae's cooking, now—

Doggone, even thinking about Ben took him back to Vera Mae. Have to try again.

Wasn't any use thinking about Mulemouth and what he was going to do when he caught up with the buckskin, 'cause too much of that was going to be decided by the stud and not by Lonnie. Wasn't any use thinking about afterwards, because that was sure an uncertain quantity.

Prince was so deadbeat that Lonnie smelled the water before the horse did, and swung the reins that way. Either it wasn't as bad alkali as the pond last night, or they were both getting used to it; Prince drank without hardly blowing first, and Lonnie thought the water in the canteen tasted fine.

He settled down again to let Prince picket on the bunch grass and salt hay. He remembered, then, the leg of jackrabbit he'd carried all day; he got it out and chewed on it without pleasure. Maybe he wouldn't have to shoot again the rest of his time down here, which was strictly limited by Prince's time. He had a lot of raisins left, and just sitting in the saddle all day didn't burn up too much food.

Trouble was, it didn't tire a man out either. If he could just go to sleep, and not think, Vera Mae wouldn't keep coming back to him.

Well, he'd lie here awhile, and then give Prince his nosebag full of barley. Make the old boy eat as much bunch grass as possible first; once he tasted the grain he'd waste his time begging for more. The desert wasn't any place for a pet.

He'd said it to Vera Mae once. The desert is for dudes. And there she came back again.

Maybe if he thought about Joan, he'd be glad he was where he was. The first trip after Mulemouth had been pure pleasure, like going deer hunting when he was a kid, before Squawberry took the edge off his meat eating. It'd been like stretching his muscles after a long, rained-in time

171

in the house. Him and old Bob, living free on the land . . .

But Prince wasn't Bob, and Joan wasn't—

No. But what he was trying to say to himself was, even if she's dead, Joan was a mean woman. Funny she'd had two such nice kids. She was just plain, dull mean, never missing a chance to whine a little, taking no pleasure from what he could do for her, not really interested in the kids, except to see they were dressed and carried their lunches to school so those other women at Salal Flats wouldn't think poorly of her.

Those women down there! Maybe they would have been all right if they'd lived in a town, like Mark said, lived where a lady had some choice of friends instead of seeing the same ones over and over again, and those not of her choice. It hadn't been long before Vera Mae saw them for—

He rubbed the back of his head against the smooth leather of the saddle seat and began to laugh. He was like old Prince there; a little petting had spoiled him. He called out, "You miss Old Man, Prince?" and then was startled at his own voice; he hadn't heard it or any other but those horses for two days. Well, he was no dude rider; in the desert, it isn't good when you get started talking to yourself or your horse.

He sang softly to himself, a song called "Detour." Singing is good, talking is bad. Start talking to yourself, and you can't stop. He didn't have to put any thought on why he'd married Joan. When he came back from the rodeo circuit, everything around that country looked so good to him that she naturally fell into it; she'd just moved up there, her father was one of the twenty fellows who'd owned the Salal Flats store in Lonnie's time. And she'd married him because why shouldn't she? He had ready money and good clothes and a brand-new Porter saddle.

He guessed it was his fault for not making it clear to her that he was through with traveling, that he was going to stick with the homestead from now on out. When she found that out, she'd soured on him, and stayed sour till

172

she sneaked out to ride Mulemouth and spoil the riding for him.

Nowadays he could think about that morning and not flinch, and that was a step forward. Since it hadn't hurt the kids, since it had, in its way, brought him—

He sat up and began drawing a map of the country around him in the sand. He used a twig of mesquite to draw with; first the big North Butte, then the Little Butte, and the alkali pond where he'd slept last night; now, the draw, as far as he'd gone down it. He left the end half brushed in, as the Forest Service had taught him to do with country he didn't actually know about, but could only guess.

All right, here he came out of the draw, and headed this way to the second alkali pond. And to the south—

He raised his head and made a reconnaissance before sketching anything at all. Eight buttes were visible, two of them so far in the distance that he couldn't tell if they were big or little. One was almost on him, about two miles away; the drainage from it was probably what forced up this pond here. And there were two more, call them Twin Buttes, about—

Something moved on the top of East Twin Butte. He sat up and swung his legs crosslegged under him. He pulled his hat down over his eyes, and after a moment took his jackknife and made a little hole in the brim with the leather punch. This served as a sort of lens, and things got clearer. The thing—animal—moved again.

He was looking southeast, sun was almost directly west. The animal—horse—was taking a spy of the country before dark.

The top of the butte wasn't level. Where he'd first seen the horse—stallion—was the top point of the tilted table top. Now the stallion walked slowly toward the low point, and Lonnie was pretty sure he could hear his mares moving around just behind and below him. Gonna take a look off that end, and see what-for . . .

173

Satisfied, the stallion broke into a trot and went down to the low end fast, and the hole in Lonnie's hat brought the scene into focus, and those were more horses coming up after him. The trot went downhill with certainty, and trotting is not the usual gait of a wild stallion.

Before he came off the Butte the stallion—Mulemouth —turned and seemed to look straight at Lonnie. Then he was gone.

LONNIE STOOD UP, and his hands were wet with sweat, which is not usual in the desert. That fool Prince hadn't seen a thing; he acted like stallions and bands of mares were nothing to him. Lonnie crammed the burlap feedbag full and tied it over Prince's head; he might not graze again that night, and he was going to need his strength.

Thereafter the man stood there and forced himself to be patient while the big horse took his own damn time about finishing the barley. Then he saddled and bridled, washing the bit and Prince's mouth out with a piece of shirt tail and water from the canteen; Prince fought, wanting to wash the good barley uselessly through his belly with water.

Lonnie rigged a hackamore under the bridle and tied its rope to his strings; if he had to stop Prince he wanted him to stop. But maybe he wouldn't have to stop him.

If it had been allowed to talk to your horse, he would have told him to do his best. Prince's life depended on working hard, working good and working fast; there weren't three days more of this kind of thing in the old boy. But it wasn't good to talk out loud to a horse on the desert, so Lonnie just thought it and got into the saddle. As soon

174

as he started riding he remembered the rabbit and pulled the leg out of his saddle bag where he'd put it back after a couple of pleasureless chaws. People who say that hunger'll make you like anything never ate barbecued jackrabbit without salt.

He finished and threw the bone far away; then he reached under the saddle blanket edge and found Prince sweathing a little already. He wiped the sweat on the hand he'd used to eat with and on his face; wiped it around the inside of the saddle bag. Hadn't meant to sneak up on Mulemouth, but if it was necessary, might as well smell like a horse; he even dropped his old leather fire jacket overboard because it had sure soaked up a lot of char in its time.

He watched it go away behind him with regret. Be colder than hell in an hour.

He trailed first one rope and then the other to make sure they were unkinked. After that he had nothing to do but sit in the saddle and be a passenger.

He found himself shaking with cold and sweating at the same time; he had to stop and get down and empty his bladder for the third time that day, which is unheard of on the desert.

Whoa, Lonnie! How do you know it was Mulemouth? 'Cause I know.

You're talking like old Ben Davis. Talking like a mule kicked you in the head. You was five, eight miles away. I'd know that action anyplace. Ain't no other horse moves just that way.

Maybe he's come off the other side of the butte and is making tracks across the desert. So I'll run him down. He's got mares and colts to graze, and I'm carrying grain for Prince. And spurs.

Maybe—

My God, Lonnie told himself under his breath, I've been talking out loud to myself. And answering myself in another voice. One of the voices had been like Tommy

Burns's, and the other sort of a phony hick voice like that fat dude—Dutcher?—had used at the rodeo the day he'd met Vera Mae.

It was all right to think about Vera Mae now, because he'd seen Mulemouth, which meant he was on his way back to Vera Mae, and with the thing he'd gone to get for her.

All right to think about her, and how she looked asleep at night, when he'd been shook awake by a noise and gone to quiet it—horse in the barn, kid losing his covers, coyote to be scared away—and she'd never waked up, sure that Lonnie would take care of her. When she was asleep like that, she didn't look a lot older than Mike.

Think about Vera Mae when the devil'd get into her, and them riding someplace, and she'd suddenly stand on her hands on the saddle, her feet just missing the overhanging branches on the truck trail up the canyon.

Or Vera Mae when she'd cooked something new and stood by the table, looking at him and the kids, and halfscared they wouldn't like it. Mostly at him . . .

When she fixed up June's hair in the morning, she always kept her mouth open a little bit, and her tongue came out of one corner of her mouth.

When he was doing a job and didn't want to be bothered, she'd come stand with hands behind her back, sort of swinging on her heels till he straightened up and gave her a quick kiss.

Man could think about Vera Mae from now till the end of the week, and never have to think the same thing twice.

The sun went down over the flat edge of the desert, and it got colder without waiting for any further invitation, but there was enough light left and plenty to see the butte he called East Twin Butte. No animal, horse or otherwise, moved on it. Mulemouth had brought his band down to graze by night. This side or the other he couldn't tell.

Prince stumbled.

Well, the old boy could be tired. He'd pick up when

176

he smelled those mares and that stud. This was why he'd brought Prince and not Bob, this and because he didn't want Bob killed. Mulemouth'd do his part for a gelding, horses didn't have good sense about that, but a gelding wouldn't do his share back again.

They weren't more than a mile from the base of the butte now. Prince stumbled again, so he hadn't picked up any scent or sound. Lonnie raised his bridle hand high, ready to catch up the bits if Prince went into a real falter.

Some old boy—maybe one of the preachers that had used the clubhouse across from the ranger station—some old boy had said once that it was man's nature to brag. So maybe he was just bragging when he thought there wasn't another woman in the world like Vera Mae. Maybe there was a million of 'em.

But he hadn't happened to run into them. Not any of the girls he or Johnny Wheelwright had fussed around with when they were traveling, not any of the wives at Salal Flats, not Joan or his mother.

Maybe if he thought about his mother he'd calm down some. He wasn't really fixed to do much thinking, the state he was in, and he might have to use his head pretty soon.

Ladies must have been different back in the days thirty years ago. You didn't run into many of the quiet ones like his mother any more. Not sulky quiet like Joan but just quiet. She'd cleaned her house and cooked her meals and tended her chickens—till Lonnie was old enough to tend them, and maybe that was why he hated chickens to this day—and she'd reared Lonnie as best she could with cattle falling from the day he was born till everything went smash and his dad got a job with the WPA.

He supposed she'd kissed him some in his time, but it was before his memory set in and got active. Just done her work and kept her mouth shut, and if sometimes Dad couldn't stand things—like when they took away the front country ranch he'd bought with his war profits—and

177

brought home a jug and got drunk, why all she'd done about it was fetch a pitcher of water from the spring so the old man wouldn't have to drink his liquor straight.

She hadn't had a drop herself, nor had it occurred to Dad to offer it to her.

I think about him ten times for once I remember her. *I ain't gonna let Vera Mae get like that.*

He had spoken aloud again, and he stopped and shoved his hat back and rubbed his forehead; sweat poured down from the band, and he rubbed it around on his face, though the wind was biting, and the cool gave him a headache. As he pulled his hat back down, Prince stopped, and Lonnie saw that he'd ridden him nose-on into the foot of the butte.

It was dark as was possible now; there'd be some moon, but not for a couple of hours. Lonnie swung the reins tight, and Prince stepped out that way. Chunks of rock had fallen off the butte and this was no place to ride in the night, but if they moved out to clearer ground, they might not find their way at all.

So Lonnie held his hand high, and to the left of the center of Prince's neck, and he carried his right leg back a little, and Prince—after all, he'd been trained for sixteen years—kept curving around the foot of the butte, walking slow and scary, frightened of the rocks, missing his stall and his supper, cut off from everything Old Man Trellis had taught him was a good stud's due.

Old Man was sure good to a horse as long as he needed him.

He tried to remember the words to "The Chisholm Trail" to say over under his breath, but they wouldn't come. Year he'd ridden rodeo they used to keep playing "Empty Saddles in the Old Corral," which was new then, and he said the words to that instead, making no noise about it.

It was all right to think about rodeo now, even if it did make him think about Vera Mae. That had been quite a

178

year, and he had met a lot of girls who were kind of like Vera Mae, which was why he turned to her the minute he met her; it was so easy to talk to her. But it didn't take long of watching her with the kids, of just seeing her, to see she was different. Maybe smarter, or maybe it was something else again. It was hard for a man to tell, but whatever it was, he sure liked it.

He'd liked those other gals too. After being a peckerwood—like one Texas gal called him—all his life, they were just something to see. Easy to talk to, and easy to kiss, and if you kissed them and then thought a second time about it, why, next day there were no hard feelings, and if it was all in fun.

Riding rodeo wasn't like anything else in the world. Fighting fire was dangerous, or breaking horses on a ranch, and maybe if he'd had good sense at thirteen, he would have thought tailing up cows in the snow with half-witted Ben Davis to help him was not just like sending off to Sears Roebuck. But when you rode in the contests, you were by God declaring yourself as ready to get killed, and every time the whistle blew for the last contest and the day was over, there was a funny feeling of being alive that you never felt any other way.

Of course, you were always alive, but did you know it?

He chuckled at this, dumb man gets out in the desert, where there's nobody within twenty miles to wonder what he's thinking, and he gets to feeling like he's smart.

Prince walked along through the night. The only reason for hanging on to the reins was to pull the old stud up if he stumbled. There wasn't a chance in the world that Prince'd take off. He wasn't going anyplace but down.

So stop feeling sorry for him, Lon Verdoux. Old Man Trellis had treated him good, but Prince had gone past his time on the Trellis ranch, and when you went past your time with Old Man, that was it. A bullet cost money, and so did a vet to cut a good old stud so he could be turned out with the cowponies. Old Man Trellis maybe would have done a job on Prince with a jackknife, but more likely he would have worried that a gelding ate a lot.

If there had been any way he could have avoided the law, Old Man would have let his new stud fight old Prince to death, and charged admission.

He wouldn't say Old Man was cruel; he just knew about a dollar. And he was right. Every year he got richer, a little more set on his ranch. Like a man about to throw a rope from the ground at a rodeo steer, Old Man had set his heels, dug his money back into his land, and there wasn't anything, from three-dollar cattle to an earthquake, was likely to take him off his place.

It was the way to be, if you could be that way. Lonnie couldn't, and there wasn't no use trying; he'd rather the kids had nice clothes and a little fun now, today, than that they had the price of the clothes, plus interest, when Lonnie died. He couldn't be like Old Man, and he didn't want Mike to be like Stan.

Lonnie knew this one thing, and counted himself lucky to know he was never likely to be shaken out of it: *if you had a hundred and sixty acres and a strong back and you were willing to learn, you could make a ranch out of that quarter-section.*

His old man had not stuck to that, and they'd nearly lost the homestead, nearly ruined it with a plough. His dad had been willing to use his strong back, but not his head. Lonnie wasn't going into anything in a hurry.

You could probably—almost certainly—plough the whole meadow to potatoes, and one year's crop would make as much as Lonnie made in ten years. New soil would grow potatoes like weeds. And then you could put all the money back into the ranch, and twice as much, and it still wouldn't be worth much; a heavy rain, a dry summer, and the sagebrush'd be walking up to the house and looking in the window.

Take it easy, take it slow, and only put on the place what belongs there.

Such as a good woman to do half your thinking and maybe a little more. And Vera Mae had told him—not in so many words—that Mulemouth was what he needed. So—

So it came back to him and Vera Mae and Mulemouth.

And here went nothing, bacause Prince was lifting his tired head and blowing, though without much conviction. When Lonnie reached down to see if his cinches were tight, he could feel ribs; the old boy was gaunted down as for as he'd go.

CHAPTER V

PRINCE HAD the reins now. He took off away from the butte in the dark, tramping down creosote bushes and the little ground-hugging brush that hung around the butte and took advantage of the water that drained off them three, four times a year.

They were walking into the wind, and Lonnie sniffed for horses once in a while, but there wasn't anything yet; Prince must have smelled or heard something, but even after all this time of not smoking, Lonnie's nose wasn't that good.

There wasn't a cloud in the sky, and Lonnie leaned back in the saddle and shoved his hat back, too, and admired the stars. The North Star in the Big Dipper, the Seven Sisters. That was Venus just rising, and looking so big you could almost see the details, and there was Mars, and that was all that Lonnie Verdoux knew about stars. Couldn't even remember where he'd learned that, though probably from some lieutenant during the war, when they had used so much military to fight the fires. Used to have some good talks on the fire line in those days.

From the stars he was going south. This time of year

sun rose and fell about due east and west. If he had Mule-mouth in the morning, if he was ready to go home, they'd come in handy, getting his bearings.

He took a little swallow of water from his canteen.

Now the moon was coming over the edge of the desert. All the land on Lonnie's left lit up; then the edge of the moon showed, and the whole desert was visible; the buttes, solid and black at night, the occasional towering cactus, the more frequent clumps of hill-of-gold, bunch grass, creosote, the occasional dense thicket of mesquite or palo-verde or ironwood.

A swift barked and was answered by a coyote, and a jack-rabbit cut across Lonnie's trail. Old Prince went along, marching like a young horse and a good one, spending the last of his strength on whatever it was that made stallions want to fight and breed and whistle. *Cojones.* But it was something more than that.

It wasn't the mares that drove studs on, Lonnie was convinced, it was the fight with the other stud to get the mares. If there wasn't any other horse around, they'd graze along in their pastures with their wives and their babies, no harder to handle than any other animal.

On the other hand, Lonnie heard, if there wasn't any mares around, you could graze a half-dozen studs in one field, like kids' ponies. He didn't know that for himself; he'd never had a pack of stallions to graze. It was true of bulls, though. He'd seen that with his own eyes.

He took a pinch of raisins and chewed them slowly, getting the last good out of them. They made his throat and stomach ache, reminded him of how little he'd had to eat. He slid his hand between his belt and his belly; me and Prince are gaunted down together.

Some of the clumps of brush out on the desert south of him seemed to be moving. There was some wind, but not enough for that. He pulled Prince down gently; the horse sort of leaned into the bit, not fighting it yet, but ready to fight if he was not allowed to move forward pretty soon.

182

The clumps moved again. They could be antelope, but if they were they were the most monstrous antelope ever seen. Could be burros—naw, ears would show even this far.

He pushed his hand forward a little, and Prince moved out. The old horse broke into a foxtrot, and Lonnie let him go. There weren't any chains on the bit to jingle, and the old saddle was broke in ten years ago; it wasn't going to creak.

The foxtrot lifted into a square trot. Lonnie sat to it so his pants wouldn't slap the saddle, and the little drink of water banged painfully around in his belly; he got a stitch in his left side that doubled him over the horn, but he put his hands flat on the pommel and shoved back.

The stitch went away. The moon came all the way up, almost rushing into the sky, and a beam caught an alkali pond near the grazing mares and sent a shaft of light back into the sky. It was sure pretty, in a dismal sort of way; the desert wasn't for him.

Now he was close enough to see that some of the big shadows had little shadows alongside them. But he couldn't see a stallion anyplace. If there had been a hill, now, the leader'd be on it, looking out. But the country was flat around there.

Mulemouth must be feeling awful sure of himself to take his band out on the flat wasteland that way. Or maybe it had been a bad summer for feed. Or maybe this was the wrong horse herd. Mulemouth was no horse to take his family into trouble.

Lonnie never did see where the big horse came from—it was Prince that saved both their lives. The first thing Lonnie knew the old stud under him was twisting and rearing all at one time, flinging himself back and up. Lonnie's knees clamped down and his right hand caught leather, and he lost a stirrup, but he was still on board when Prince ended up pointed the other way.

Mulemouth looked bigger than a house on his hind legs, his golden belly shining in the moonlight. He hung up there, and it seemed like years; breath whistled through the square nostrils. Prince was trying to get up, to meet him; and Lonnie found his body wanted to get out of that saddle, hit the dirt and roll for safety.

He fought himself calm and got a lass' rope from its thongs, and lashed out at the mile-high stretch of golden skin with the coiled rope. Mulemouth faltered, and Lonnie lifted his reins high and swung Prince to the left, then kicked his spurs home hard.

The old horse stumbled coming around; this was where his stiff legs hurt. But he kept his footing and plunged forward.

The huge hoof seemed to miss Lonnie's hat brim so close he could feel its wind, but it must have been farther away because it never touched Prince's rump.

Lonnie put Prince into a run and made as small a circle as he thought the lame legs could manage. Mulemouth came after them, and he was heavy enough and straight-legged with anger to make the soft desert ground thunder. He sank his teeth into Prince's rump, and held on, buck-jumping after Prince with his two hind feet off the ground, and all his weight on his teeth.

Prince struggled to get his legs around and fight back, but Lonnie held his head straight, and his spurs hooked, and beat at Mulemouth's face and ears with the coiled rope. It stung, and Mulemouth let go.

Lonnie lined Prince straight into the banded mares. They whickered with excitement as the strange stallion went by, but they didn't run; by now, Lonnie must just about smell and look like a horse. Mulemouth thundered after them, but he was getting mighty tentative; that rope hurt, and all he wanted was to get this strange horse out of his band.

Lonnie and Prince went right through the band, and stopped, and Mulemouth reared to threaten them; this time Lonnie let the uncoiled end of the rope, with its stiff leather and metal honda, flick right into Mulemouth's face

184

while he was at the height of his rear. The buckskin went off balance and fell backward but he landed on his feet like a cat. He blew, all four feet spraddled, ready to attack again.

Lonnie rode Prince off a half a mile; the old boy was glad to go. He'd had enough of fighting, enough of courting those mares, to last him a while.

Mulemouth trailed after them, not attacking so long as the other stud was going away from the lady-horses.

When Mulemouth was giving them enough distance, Lonnie reached into one saddle bag with his hand and got out a handful of barley. He fed it to Prince from the saddle, reaching forward and holding his hand between the sidebars of the bit. Prince wasn't too blowed to eat.

Then Lonnie used the other hand to get out the bottle of blue gall remedy and daub some on the wound on Prince's rump.

He'd proved what he'd come here to prove: a good man on an old stud can fight a good stud and no man. The first round had gone to him, and he sat easy in the saddle, slipping Prince a little grain now and then, and only moving him forward when Mulemouth dropped his head to try and snaffle some bunch grass. Every time Prince went toward Mulemouth—and toward the mares—the buckskin head came up, and Mulemouth snorted.

There was a pretty good belly on the wild stallion. But if Prince could stand up another twenty-four hours, hunger'd be making Mulemouth pay.

Lonnie prepared to wait him out.

THERE WASN'T any moonset that night; she was on the wane, and rode right into the blue sky of dawn. There wasn't any dew either, and Mulemouth hadn't had a single bite since moonup; and no water. The mares moved down to the alkali pond at false dawn, and Lonnie drifted his horse slowly after them. Mulemouth could run after his ladies, then turn and face the slowly drifting Prince, then go after the mares again; but he never got his head to the ground.

Lonnie dumped half a canteen load into his hat and watered Prince; and all the time the big old boy got his palmful of grain. Food and water might be the equalizer against Mulemouth's youth and toughness. Or it might not.

But the buckskin was off balance; dawn caught him still down on the flat, and not up on the butte, safe. Daylight almost never found the wild horses on the flat.

Today was different. The mares were nervous and uncertain; the way of a broomtail with love would disgust you with all females, and these were worked up about the new stallion. Mulemouth would whistle at them and move out. Then he'd see that only a third of his mares were following him, and he'd come back.

About two-thirds of the mares had colts at their sides, running all the way from wobbly-legged fall foals to spring-born fellows near as big as their maws, ready to wean. They ran every color of the horse book, with pintos and grulla sort of ahead. Which showed that Mulemouth hadn't gotten back his old band, from which Lonnie'd stolen him; the foals in it had been almost all palominos and buckskins.

A horse is no more a one-harem man than a man is a

186

one-woman man. Mulemouth, breaking over the ridge, had just fought and killed—or driven off—the first stallion he'd met, and taken his band.

Lonnie found a few odd raisins in his shirt pocket and chewed them. They tasted of salt. Something in the Bible about eating your own sweat, but there wasn't any time to worry about that.

Mulemouth was losing his temper. Being trapped on the flat had something to do with it, but having his mares roll their eyes and twitch around Prince had a lot more. And going without food or water didn't help.

He was rushing Prince every few minutes now. But Prince wasn't acting like a wild stud; spurs and rein ends took him out of Mulemouth's reach in a dead run; that first bite had been the only one Mulemouth had gotten in. The big buck would come snorting and charging, and then make an eleven on the ground as he came to a stop, realizing that Prince was drawing him away from the mares; he'd head back, and here would come Prince again, sidling up, making noises like a farm boy at a Sunday school picnic.

Those runs weren't doing Prince any good. They weren't hurting Mulemouth any in the body, but they were sure playing hell with his peace of mind. Pretty soon he'd stop thinking.

When Lonnie'd been about ten years old somebody'd told him that it was a damn poor man couldn't outthink a horse. He couldn't remember who it was but he sure hoped whoever it was had a reputation for truthfulness.

He made his plans. Pretty soon Mulemouth was going to get desperate, and do something unpredictable, like run for the butte with what mares he could get; or keep on in one of his charges till he ran Prince down and killed him. Once the wild stud lost his temper completely, a little thing like getting stung with a honda wasn't going to stop him.

On the edge of the alkali pond there were a half-dozen

mesquite bushes. They weren't very strong, but they grew pretty close together; maybe they'd cinch down to a snubbing post. But not for a certainty.

Lonnie slipped his gloves out of his hip pocket and put them on. His hands had swollen from the alkali, and he hadn't worn gloves for over a day; but he managed to wriggle into them. Then he swung his legs and headed Prince straight for the pond and the middle of the mares, standing around on three legs, waiting to see how this came out, who their new boss was.

Mulemouth stood off, his square nostrils blowing and showing red, his head cocked a little on one side, figuring this out. Prince was nervous at going away from the buckskin; the dried blood on his rump showed he'd been bitten deep last night, and a horse has a good memory.

But you don't obey spurs and reins for sixteen years and then quit in a day.

Lonnie skirted as close to the bushes as he could get, and still Mulemouth held his ground. He trumpeted, but he didn't move; and this was the payoff, because there was always a chance he might run for it now, when most of the mares were between him and the strange stallion.

Alkali crackled under Prince's hoofs. Lonnie got a rope ready and built up a loop. He hadn't thought there was any sweat left in him, but he'd been wrong; it broke out now between his shoulder blades, cold and crawling down his spine.

The ground thundered, and Mulemouth charged.

Lonnie trailed his loop and held Prince with his back to the buckskin; Prince fretted, but like Old Man had said, he'd been a hell of a stock horse in his day.

As Mulemouth reared to strike, Lonnie threw, underhand. He wasn't the roper that Vera Mae was, but she'd a been proud of him; the loop settled around Mulemouth's neck.

Lonnie swung his legs, and he could almost feel the blood spurt out of Prince's sides; the old boy went forward

188

in a buck that knocked Lonnie's belly into the horn. Then he was swinging his left leg back again and jerking on the reins enough to break a horse's jaw, and here they went around the bushes.

Mulemouth came after them, the loop loose on his neck, and Lonnie dived off, grabbing his carbine from the boot, and holding the rope end in his other hand. He let go of Prince's reins, and hoped to God the horse didn't go too far before the split ends fell and ground-tied him from habit.

He went back around the bushes on foot, and raised the carbine in the air with his left hand and pulled the trigger.

The mares scattered from hell to breakfast and Mulemouth went back against the rope so fast that Lonnie hardly had time to make a tie in the rope.

Then he dropped the gun to the alkali—he'd had it since he was fifteen—and looked around for Prince.

The good old horse had ground-tied himself ten feet away.

The noise of Lonnie's seat hitting the saddle was almost as loud as the gun had been. He jerked up his lines and made a charge, and the second rope came free and flew through the air—and missed.

Mulemouth was going toward the bushes loosening the loop, about to get free—

The tight gloves almost kept him from trailing his lass' back in and coiling again. But they were good ropes—Vera Mae'd seen to that—and he rebuilt and threw—and Mulemouth turned and charged at this new hurt—and the first rope was tight, the second one ran clean from Mulemouth's neck to the dallies on the horn—and there was one stud wasn't going no place for a while.

Lonnie tied fast and got out of the saddle. Prince was stock horse enough to keep a line tight to his horn, and even if he wasn't, he'd had enough of getting close to Mulemouth.

The ropes tightened and Mulemouth's breath began to

189

go as they strangled him. He'd pull toward the bushes, and Prince's line'd tighten; he'd pull toward Prince, and the line to the bush would hold. He'd rear, and they'd both get him.

Mulemouth decided to stand still.

Lonnie went over and picked up his carbine and looked it over. It was a little banged up, but nothing he couldn't fix. He rubbed alkali off with his sleeve and looked out at the mares, timidly beginning to rejoin the studs, and he grinned. He put the gun back in its boot, but he didn't remount. He was shaking so bad he might scare Prince if he touched him.

So he sat on his heels and wished he had some tobacco.

Mulemouth was sure getting red in the eye. He was getting madder and madder, too; and the madder he got, the more he forgot about the bushes and tried to get to Prince.

One bush came up by the roots, and Lonnie stood up. There wasn't anything he could do about the shaking in his legs; he'd just have to let them shake. He went over and took two short lengths of rope—just clothesline—out of his saddle bags, and now they were empty except for a couple of handfuls of grain. He'd cut it pretty close. Prince looked like hell.

He tied a length of rope to each side of Prince's romal, let them fall. They might make the horse think he was ground-tied, for a while at least. Then he took Prince's bridle off.

He wiped the foam off on his shirt, and he took a fistful of grain, and he started walking up on Mulemouth. He'd never had to do anything as bad as this in his life, but neither had the man who made the first parachute jump.

The stud didn't like any part of it. He'd had no food or water for a day, and no air for maybe five minutes, but there was a hell of a lot of fight left in him. He struck at Lonnie with a big front hoof, and Lonnie jumped clear. Wasn't much fight left in him, either.

190

Lonnie made a second jump and got an arm around Mulemouth's neck. The big neck bowed, and the teeth snapped a couple of inches from Lonnie's thigh, but the ropes held. Lonnie's hand began inching the rolled-up bridle along Mulemouth's neck.

That was the tallest horse, and him not anxious to wear Lonnie's best bridle. But maybe all the days in the breaking corral told; Lonnie got to the stud's crest with his fist, and let the bridle roll down Mulemouth's face, and said good-by to his fingers as he slid the other hand up to press the teeth apart.

The bridle slid home, and Lonnie buckled it, and there was Mulemouth, a saddle horse. Except he didn't have no saddle on, and he was wearing two loops around his neck.

Lonnie went back and sat on his heels some more.

Prince was holding. Maybe he wasn't really ground-tied. Maybe he was just trying to stay away from Mulemouth.

The bushes weren't holding so good, though. Another root had come up.

Lonnie went to them, and tried to untie the knot. But Mulemouth had jerked it too tight for his fingers. He took his knife and cut it, and thought what hell he'd catch from Vera Mae. It was a little like rolling a cigarette with a leaf from a preacher's Bible. He took a firm hold of the rope with both hands and started going up it, hand over hand.

Mulemouth was pulling, and Lonnie's heels slid a little. But every foot Mulemouth made, old Prince took up the slack, and they went across the desert, foot by foot, with Lonnie getting six inches closer to Mulemouth for every foot he was dragged.

He got a hand on Mulemouth's neck, and he brought his rope in with the other hand and tied a quick noose around the buckskin's nose, and threw the line over the back, and caught it from under. Mulemouth went up, and when he came down, Lonnie was in front of him; when he pulled on the rope, it choked Mulemouth's nose and pressed around his belly too. It was the best tie he knew.

There never was a horse—except a locoed one—who wouldn't follow that tie.

The trouble was, he couldn't lead Mulemouth and get to Prince at the same time. The stock horse kept moving away, like he'd been trained all his life; Prince, when there's a rope on your horn, keep it tight.

Lonnie looked the situation over. It didn't look too favorable. About like having a bear by the tail, like they said.

He had his stud. No question about it, there was Mulemouth with a bridle on, and a real crackup lead rope, to boot. And Lonnie had some rope left, enough to make a short loop and a throw.

Only trouble was, there wasn't anything to throw at. He could catch up one of Mulemouth's front feet and pull it up to his belly; but a half-wild horse like that would fight the rope till it tore his foot off. A three-legged stud, now, wasn't much good.

If he had another man along, even a little bitty old man—

But there was no use in looking out along the desert.

He grinned suddenly. If that had been a deer he shot the carbine off at, a game warden'd be right here, giving him a ticket.

Well, he'd known this when he started out. Wasn't anybody'd be interested in a damn-fool horse hunt like this, except Vera Mae. She'd have come, but if they'd both been killed, what would have happened to the kids?

Now, she was just the gal he'd like to see coming across the flats. Vera Mae probably could rope Mulemouth's tail, and that would do it. Tie the tail to the head, and let the horse go around till he falls down, and when he gets up he's real gentle for a few minutes.

But he'd never been a trick roper, and he didn't think

Mulemouth and Prince'd stand like that while he went off and practiced. Anyway—

There was one thing for it, and he sure hated to do it! He was going to look damn funny flying across the desert with his stomach hanging out of his mouth; it was already tickling his Adam's apple.

Lonnie took his gloves off, with regret. Handling all that rope a man could get a hand sawed in half. He unbuttoned his shirt and pulled out the tails.

If he'd thought to bring hobbles—

He coiled the rope at his belt, and put the end in his teeth.

He took off from a crouch. The minute he landed on Mulemouth's back, he knew that the buckskin was not going to co-operate. That stud could sure stand a lot of choking.

His hind end left the ground, and Lonnie nearly left his back. He caught on by the mane. Mulemouth brought his head back, and the bit bars were about all that saved Lonnie's leg from being bitten in two. Even so he lost some pants leg, a lot of skin, and a little flesh. The pain was enough to make a man throw up, but he had hold of the mane—and he continued to hold on to it till his head cleared.

Mulemouth reared, and that was his mistake. He'd gotten by all his life by using his front feet on other studs, but Lonnie was no stud. When the horse was on his hind feet, Lonnie made a wild grab for the reins and the lead line, and jumped off again, and Mulemouth hit the ground with a bang.

Before he could get up, Lonnie was sitting on his head.

There wasn't much more to it. He whipped his shirt off, and when it seemed like a good time, he got it around a thrashing front fetlock. He pulled on the sleeves. Something ripped, but the shirt held; he let go a little bit when Mulemouth kicked out, tightened up a whole lot more when the hoof came toward him, and slipped his little loop over the shirt. Now he could really pull, and now his hands missed their gloves; the rope bit through his calloused palm.

But he tied a good square knot from the hoof to the belly-lead line, and got off; not like a lady getting out of a buggy, but just as far as he could in one jump from a horse's head; if they ever made that a rodeo event, he bet he could be All-American.

Mulemouth struggled to his feet, and stood on three legs. He looked kind of safe.

Lonnie ran his hand over his mouth, and went and unsaddled Prince. When the noose came away from Mulemouth's neck, the big buckskin took a deep breath and tried to run, but he was making no speed. Lonnie overtook him on foot, and pulled him around with the reins; Mulemouth hardly tried to bite him.

Lonnie threw the saddle on and took time to get the blanket smooth; he cinched up.

Then he went and slid off Prince's headstall, and the old boy was free. He shook himself and ran and rolled, and went to the alkali lake and drank, and then started chasing the mares.

Mulemouth looked after his successor, and didn't do anything about it.

Lonnie got on board. Mulemouth staggered a little on his three legs, but stood; he just gave a little rear to show he was still about the best stud on the desert.

Lonnie cut the square knot, after he'd run the slack end over his horn and dallied.

There was a good rough ride ahead, but nothing he wouldn't live through. A little sunfishing, and a little bucking, and maybe a little rearing over backwards, but Lonnie'd already proved he was a real good jumper.

And there was the rope down to the front foot that he could always pull up on if he wanted a rest.

It would be a shame to take day wages for a job like this.

194

THERE WAS a little haze over the meadow; not really a fog, but enough mist to spread the moonlight out, make it shine evenly on everything without throwing much shadow. Down in the beaver pond the beavers were as busy as beavers, he could hear their tails slapping.

Lonnie was sure glad that Mulemouth didn't have any shoes on. He rode right up to the front porch, and got down, and tied his lead rope to one of the porch supports. His dad had sure larruped him plenty for doing that when he was a kid, and he had bawled out Mike and June for it often enough; but he just felt like doing a bad thing tonight.

Anyway, no harm'd come of it. Mulemouth was too well broke to pull back on his lines, and not educated enough to chew on a hitching post.

Lonnie sat down on the edge of the porch and took off his boots. He left them out there, and opened the front door real quiet, and went in the kitchen and lit the kerosene stove without making a light. When the coffee began to smell, he set fire in a coal-oil lamp. He carried it and a cup of coffee into the bedroom, and set the coffee down on the little table between his and Vera Mae's bed.

Vera Mae came awake all in a rush. She said, "Oh, Lonnie!" and then she got a grip on herself, and her voice quieted down. "Didn't expect you back till morning."

He put the lamp down next to the coffeecup. "Brought you a cup of coffee."

He thought she was going to scream. When he put the lamp down she got a good look at him, and he'd forgotten what he must look like. Riding all day without a shirt

195

across the desert had raised blisters on his shoulders and back, and his face was all whiskers where it wasn't alkali and dried sweat. And Mulemouth had just about eaten his pants off.

"This is where I wish I'd finished that bathroom," he said. "A little water'd make me look like a gentleman."

"I'll run you a bath," Vera Mae said. She got out of bed, and the lamplight shone through her nightgown, and she was sure pretty.

Lonnie got taken aback a little. "You'll do what?"

She went out into the hall, and then he heard a noise he'd waited a long time to hear. The noise of water running into a bathtub. He hurried after her.

Where the hall used to end in a blank wall a door had been cut. Through the door he could see steam. He pushed Vera Mae aside and looked in. His mail-order bathtub was filling up as fast as any in the country; his mail-order toilet was ready to use, and so was his washbasin, and there was linoleum on the floor and a mirror over the washstand. There was a window with frosted glass too.

"Doggone," he said. "You never."

"I just cooked," she said. "Mark and Stan and Andy, Clint and some of the other boys did the work. Tommy bossed."

"Tommy?" he asked. He took his undershirt off and started to hang it on a hook on the door. On second thought he opened the window and threw it out. He threw his socks and pants and underpants after it. His shirt had worn off Mulemouth's hoof by noon.

"Tommy nearly went crazy when he found out where you'd gone," Vera Mae said. It sure made him feel good to see her eyes and know she was making fun of him. He slid into the tub, and it was so hot it burned him. Vera Mae handed him the soap. "Tommy came up here looking for you and Mark. He had an awful fight with the regional office about that supervisor down there, running his fire so that Tommy's two best men quit. When he heard you'd

196

headed for the desert, he was all for trying to get the Forest Service to send a plane after you. I talked him out of it."

The water was finding about ten sore and cut places he hadn't known he had. "You did, huh?"

"I figured," Vera Mae said, "if you wanted to go back with them next year, you could or you couldn't. That's your business. But I wasn't going to let them do favors for you, and expect to get paid back . . . Tommy and Andy worked on their lieu days, and Dot and I cooked. Just a personal favor. Worked all day and all night to surprise you."

He scrubbed soap into his hair, and ducked out of the water. "Don't think one bath'll get me clean," he said. "I'll get up later and take another . . . Those kids sure sleep sound."

"Well, they haven't been worried," Vera Mae said, "like I have."

Lonnie stood up and reached for a bath towel. Now he had a hot-water heater, he'd build him a laundry room out back. With a gasoline motor on the washing machine. "You been worried?" he asked.

"Yes," Vera Mae said. "I sure have. The thermostat on the new water heater wasn't working right. But I think I got it fixed."

"Doggone," Lonnie said. "You hardly need a man around here at all."

Vera Mae said, "That's what you think." She opened a brand-new cupboard, and took out a pair of shorts. She handed them to him, and he put them on. He'd never felt so clean in his life.

"Say," he said, "I don't want to get dressed again. Put my horse away, will you?"

She nodded and went toward the front of the house. He followed her, and when she opened the front door, he realized he hadn't dried good; the night wind was sure cold. But the moon and that mist together sure made a good light for showing off a buckskin horse.

"Oh, Lonnie," Vera Mae said. "My God, Lonnie, isn't he beautiful."

"He'll do," Lonnie said, "till we can catch us a better one."

Vera Mae was out in the dirt in her nightgown, running all around Mulemouth, looking him over. She stood up, laughing out loud.

"Soon's I get my pants on," Lonnie said, "I'll get your saddle. You'll want to try him out."

She came back into the house and looked at him. He couldn't tell what kind of an expression she had on her face, because there wasn't any light in the hall, and her back was to the moonglow.

He went into the bedroom and pulled on a pair of levis out of the closet. He stepped into boots without socks.

He had it to do, and he sure didn't want to. But it would be easier if he didn't face her. "I was yellow," he said, from the bedroom, pretending to himself it took all this time to button his pants. "After I got you, I couldn't stand the idea of making you a widow, is why I never went back for him. Then I saw how it was, and there's your horse. I figure you better take him over. You're more up on rodeos and things, and I'll make you a trailer, and we can take him to the shows until he gets well-known. With what you know, he ought to be State Champion Roping Horse in a year."

She said, "Thanks, Lonnie."

"Sure," he said. "Thanks for finishing the bathroom . . . I gotta tell you about Prince. Left him on the desert with a bunch of broomtails. He'll never make out on desert feed, but I didn't have the heart to shoot him. And me with my carbine along."

"Sure," Vera Mae said.

"He'll get sick of it pretty soon, and come up the desert trail home. Means he'll bring that pack of worthless broomtails with him and we'll have to drive them back. Be a chore."

198

"Sure," Vera Mae said.

"We'll do it together," Lonnie said. "The kids can help."

"I ought to go wake them," Vera Mae said. "To see Mulemouth."

"Naw," Lonnie said. "Let it go till morning. We'll put him in his old breaking corral with some hay, and then you and I got some things to talk over, and the kids might be in the way."

"I've been thinking," Vera Mae said.

Lonnie said, "Yeah?"

"No use my getting dressed just for a few minutes," she said. "You take Mulemouth down to his corral."

"Sure," Lonnie said.

"On account of, I'll have plenty of time to try him out."

"Sure," Lonnie said. "The rest of your life."